Arson

THE GERMAN LIST

LAURA FREUDENTHALER

Arson

TRANSLATED BY
TESS LEWIS

LONDON   NEW YORK   CALCUTTA

Seagull Books, 2025

First published in German as *Arson*
by Laura Freudenthaler

© Jung und Jung, Salzburg, 2023

First published in English translation by Seagull Books, 2025
English translation © Tess Lewis, 2025

ISBN 978 1 8030 9 561 5

British Library Cataloguing-in-Publication Data
A catalogue record for this book is available from the British Library.

Typeset by Seagull Books, Calcutta, India

If the keeper of the flame goes berserk,
so does fire.

Stephen J. Pyne

A wide road rising, its highest point a picture framed by buildings, the backdrop a section of a massive round stone edifice. From the left enters a small group led by a tour guide, walking backwards and carrying a standard. He turns and disappears into the right edge of the picture, followed by the group. Shouts swell, a crowd enraptured by the sound of their voices, then ebb away. I wake up and don't know where I am. Day is as far behind me as it is to come. I've slept a transitional sleep and feel alien. My limbs are splayed, from the centre out I find my way back. I move one leg, pull the other in, lift my right hand, touch my hip, my forehead, then prop myself up on my forearm. Try to discern and construe lines in the darkness. After a while, the bottom of the window turns out to be the edge of a table, above me a beam emerges from the blackness that is thickest in the corners, which are connected by walls that make up this room, from which a hallway leads to the main room where the front door is. For several weeks now I've been in this landscape, in which houses are sparsely scattered and solitary. The sound must have woken me. Something's prowling. The cat waiting for dawn when it will be fed.

Prowling is not a sound. At this hour, nothing and no one is waiting. There are some who endure and some who are in their element. Mornings, the cat waits at a safe distance until I go back into the house before it will approach to eat. No sense of familiarity. I lay my head back on the pillow, pull my knees to my chest, and pull the thin blanket tighter. Too late, the sleep that shielded me has dropped away. I don't belong here. There are wolves in the area. They've returned and are growing in number. They move silently and easily, their shoulder blades rising and falling under their fur with every step, they're rarely seen. On my cheek, I feel the touch of the mosquito that woke me. When I don't sleep, I become a monster. I want to insert a plug that will poison the air in the room. I leave the bedroom, go down the hall and turn on the ceiling light. In the centre of the room, motionless, is a spider as big as the palm of my outstretched hand with prey in its jaws. Neither of us moves. I lower my head. My bare feet on the tile floor. I turn off the light and get back in bed. My circle for the night is drawn by my rounded back and my bent arms and legs drawn in. The mosquito lands on my right shoulder.

I'm standing in front of the house, my left arm stretched across my chest so I can scratch my right shoulder. There was a fire in the field below, smoke rises from black piles and the wind blows it east over the open expanse. A dog comes running from the opposite direction, like a stray wisp of smoke moving with the wind. I raise my hand to my forehead to shade my eyes. The sky is white, a single cloud is as difficult to discern as the sun behind the cloud cover. The dog trots along the field path, the tracks of wheels and feet are old and dried. The dog belongs to a man with white hair. More than age has taken every unnecessary movement and any haste from him; other than stoicism, he has nothing left to share. The man who belongs to the dog has nothing to serve his guest. There's no wine, no bread, no water. Nothing but the paths leading through the flat landscape, over which they walk together—ground that no longer yields anything.

Before it gets dark, I go down and look for pockets of embers; among the ashes I find a few pieces of wood turned to coals, still warm, and cover them with earth. Rex Nemorensis is what they called the king of the wood, who was an escaped slave and murderer because he could only become king by killing the old one. The freedom to be killed one day—which could be any day. The bar on the main square is called the Golden Bough and the region is known for the forest and the strawberries that grow in it. A climate in which mistletoe also thrives. But oaks no longer do, the oak trees are dying here as they are elsewhere. I drive back to the city, back north.

It has grown cold. As if immersed in liquid metal, I feel an icy coating when I move. Not knowing where you are when you wake up, assumes a conception of space and your own body. I realize that I'm sitting upright and looking straight ahead. The constant effort to get your bearings is the least of it. You need to have seen the place where you wake up before or to understand that you've woken up in a place you don't know. You need to know that you've slept. I don't know how long I've been sitting in bed, looking ahead of me, but now I'm aware again that there are long and short spans of time. I've slept and woken up. I'm freezing.

The provisions have been used up, whatever's left is hard to come by. I have to start surviving. I pull on the wool socks lying near me. Next to the bed is a pair of sturdy shoes. The thick socks make it hard to get them on, but I manage. The nocturnal streets are empty, the air cold and dry. The ground here is under seal. In the forest, the ground is damp; in the forest there are streams and springs. I have to get to the forest. On the corner up ahead, next to the closed supermarket, there's an iron-barred gate through which a shadow disappears, slender and silent. On all fours. In the dark night, I have to overcome my instincts to kneel on the pavement, my torso upright, my cold kneecaps on the asphalt. Animals smell the water and catch my scent. I have to follow their tracks. I let myself drop onto my hands, a strain in my tendons. Let's go.

Once she was old enough, Andrea stopped spending Christmas with her family. Her boyfriend's name is Andrés; he's visiting his family in Spain. Miriam's girlfriend works during the holiday season. Her colleagues are grateful to her for her taking the shift. She spends as little time as possible in the flat she shares with her mother, who is dependent on her and with whom she speaks only when absolutely necessary. Miriam only knows about that flat second hand. When she and her girlfriend get together, they meet at Miriam's. Andrea has bought expensive wine. She opens another bottle. We talk about government benefits and getting paid off the books, and Andrea says that she could use a little lightheartedness this evening. There's chocolate cake for dessert. Andrea talks about an exhibition she'd like to have. A woman obsessed with self-portraits, with finding the one photograph that shows her the way she sees herself. It's an impossible perspective. And so, Andrea wants to duplicate each photograph she takes of herself and juxtapose the copies. The windows are open wide, it's a mild evening. We pause when the sirens are close and start talking again when the howling fades again. Miriam asks if I feel at home in my new flat. So far, I do. Andrea laughs. She puts on some Spanish music and raises her glass. To the life that uses us up. Miriam sings along with the music and Andrea invites me to dance. She puts her hands on my hips and we dance, belly to belly, in an embrace.

Mornings, I sit at my desk with a pencil in hand and keep my eyes lowered. Shadowy figures in the upper edge of my field of vision, a constant illusion—there, on the horizon, is where they'd be. The horizon divides the observable from the unobservable. When I look up, the figures disappear and only reappear above the paper. I try to expand my field of vision a bit higher and then a bit more. My hand holds the pencil, I keep the connection, lift my gaze to the window, to the street outside, farther.

The transition between heaven and earth. I try not to look into the distance but instead to see as much of the atmosphere as possible. The air begins to dance, it's the waves in space and the blood in my body. The movement behind my eyes, on my eardrums, under my skin and outside me. A glare, tiny, bright dots that won't stay still, not even for an instant. I look away in order to see deeper into space. Flakes of soot are like snowflakes, no two are exactly alike, and even smaller are the seed crystals that ascend to the stratosphere and make the clouds look especially bright. Cold air makes the bronchial tubes contract. In Australia they place wet towels around the doors so the smoke can't seep in. Fifty-one degrees Celsius outside, where the day is luminous while you're dreaming. The largest air tankers are called water bombers and can carry fifteen tonnes. I don't ask where they take the water from.

You should take a plane. Andrea urges me to indulge myself with a flight. But all that's over with in any case, I say. Then think of it as a farewell holiday. I fly to a Caribbean island with Ulrich, he bought the plane tickets, booked a flat, seventh floor, with ocean views. At the check-in desk, I hand the receptionist my credit card. I insist, I say in German to Ulrich, who's standing next to me, and I confirm my nationality in English. I don't understand you, Ulrich says in the lift on our way up to our room. We go to bed without having seen anything of our surroundings. It was already dark when we landed. I wake up in a large room filled with light. Play with the fingers of one hand, feel one arm too many on my chest. I open my eyes. Two arms on a strange bedsheet. I move both hands. Stretch one foot out behind me, my bare toes in the air. I sit up on the edge of the bed and flinch when fingers touch my back. Really? Ulrich moves closer. So late already?

As on every morning, we drink coffee on the patio and Ulrich reads yesterday's newspaper. I go inside to get milk. I close the refrigerator and pause in front of it, the carton of milk in my hand. I'm telling you for the third time, there's something under the refrigerator. Along with the darkness, nocturnal sounds and the ocean breeze waft through the open patio door. Ulrich says that's the sound of mould growing on cheese rinds and breadcrumbs. We sit next to each other on the couch, a bottle of wine and two glasses on the table. He drinks from one and says, you can hear the mycelium grow because you're so in tune with nature. In the middle of the room, the waves break against the sounds in the flat.

There's something there, I say. We're lying in bed, and Ulrich gets up and goes into the kitchen. He turns on the light and says, now I'm kneeling on the floor, now I'm looking under the refrigerator. But I don't believe him because I can tell that he doesn't want to hear what I hear. He has turned off the light and come back to the bedroom. The darkness isn't complete. I can see him. He says, nothing there. He stands next to the bed and touches my bare toes with his fingertips. I know what it is, I say, it's mice. Nonsense. Ulrich hates rodents, he's afraid of their germs and faeces. He paces back and forth between the bed and door. He says, what a fuss you're making. I can hear the rustling over his pacing. I stand on the bed, taking unsteady steps on the mattress while he marches through the room from the door to the bed and back again. I'm telling you, there's something there and it's mice, I say louder and louder. And more and more sternly he says, you're not to say that, it's not your text! I jump up and down on the mattress, there's something there. I hop back and forth, it's mice, I yell, and because the mattress is so soft, I fall over and am suddenly on my back. Ulrich rushes to the bed and puts his hand over my mouth. He lays down on top of me, to cover me completely.

Do you want more coffee? Oh yes, I say so quickly and in such a friendly voice that Ulrich looks at me, disconcerted, then right back at his newspaper. He forgets the coffee. He reads with intense concentration and I watch him from the side, wondering if he's just pretending to be unaware.

Really? I flick the words from the back of my hand with my fingernail. Why? Because they don't make sense. I've left Ulrich. I have to laugh. There really is a difference between 'I laugh' and 'I have to laugh', isn't there? Andrea asks if something happened. I don't want to see him any more and don't want to hear from him, no phone calls, news, text messages, emails, none of that. The fine particulates are still suspended in the air, I can see them as a haze in the backlight. Your and his story always had something elusive about it, as if it could end at any moment. Every story can end at any moment or be broken off because of aversion or the narrator's death or as retribution. Our story went on too long. Constant aloofness is still aloofness, Andrea says. I picture Ulrich marching back and forth between the door and the bed. You shouldn't say that. What? I'm sorry, that's not what I wanted to say. A memory. Aloofness doesn't make sense either. There can certainly be a correlation between aloofness and a feeling of meaninglessness, Andrea says. What does meaninglessness feel like? Particulate matter is not a feeling, you only feel its effects. A lot of time can pass before its negative impact on your health becomes evident. I say boredom, and, inurement. Andrea's therapist says that relationships need common projects in order to grow. Just as each individual needs goals in life.

Every flat I move into has a table where I work, eat and drink. On the floor around it lies anything I'm not using at the moment. In my right hand I hold the pencil, which I put down so that I can stretch my arm out over the table to reach for the coffee cup. While I drink, I look at my left hand resting in a loose fist on the table. In every flat there's a mattress on the floor, two quilts, two pillows.

From sleep, I twist into wakefulness, one arm stretched out behind me. I bring with me whatever I can salvage. I go to the table, my fist loose, if I squeeze hard it will all disperse. The figures from last night are dark today, their faces indistinguishable, one hunched figure paces back and forth in the shadows. When I lead the memory across the divide, I already know that there are no words for it here. The language from over there never survives the transition. I can bring images and replicate them by writing them down. I can only work with what I have. 'Darkness' and 'shadows', I write, 'forms' and 'hunched', 'hollow'; the graphite is the connection, I hold my pencil until night has retreated too far from me. At noon, I head inland. I clear the papers from the table onto the floor and from the floor I pick up a pocket diary, my computer and other papers, and put them on the table. I make phone calls, buy groceries, say hello, answer emails, read the paper, order a coffee, go to a dinner.

Locally caught fish are carved onto seven plates. You can only eat saltwater fish with a clear conscience if you're near the water. I turn to look behind me. Once again, I'm standing with my back facing inland. The night rolls in from ahead of us, a first wave is so close that I pull my foot back before stretching my leg out again as far as I can under the table, on which my hand rests holding a serrated knife with a black plastic handle. And how are you? I look around, I nod, I lift a piece of fish to my mouth on the knife, I feel the serrations on my tongue, I'm thirsty. I hold my glass out towards the pitcher of water, someone fills it, I thank him with a nod, I smile. People talk over each other, laugh, make noise. At night, the water presses against the shore. It sinks from above and rises from the depths, a relentlessly stratifying column.

I've stretched out in bed; I've turned off the light and laid my head on the pillow. The sound of motors, sirens, passers-by, how are you, voices from the day, fading away little by little. The silence deepens until the dead of night, whether or not anyone hears it. Silence is measured in thickness and depth. As is evident in the comparison of water and night, neither is a human element. Humans can't see or breathe there. A creaking of ships' masts, the tendons in my shoulder with each breath. I slide off the mattress, closer still, lay on my stomach, my head to the side, my ear on the floor. The water rolls, it works away at the hulls, at the wooden posts, the piles and supports that humans have driven into the ground and anchored there. There's a grating sound in my head.

A rockslide is heralded by noises that seem to come from above. Rock faces, crevices, peaks and ledges, jackdaw cries, scraping, trickling. The brightness increases—blinded by the light, I want to shut my eyes, I wake and am in the day. Yet another caving accident, the fifth in just a few weeks. In the abandoned salt mines, old ore tunnels, worlds of crystal, this time a cave with an underwater lake. Unnoticed, the rock had loosened, boulders fell on visitors who had been guided below ground in great numbers for many years. The crust is moving, mountains are working. It may be related to the rising temperatures in addition to atmospheric changes inside the mountain from breath and body heat. We have a false idea of eternal stone. Also, there are things we know nothing about taking place in much deeper layers.

Radiant spring weather, the first heat has arrived. The west wind pushes warm air into the city along the broad waterway. From the bridge, I look down at the river below me, extremely distinct in the bright sunlight, its small waves stiffening every few moments, every blink of the eye an image. The new grass gleams on the elongated island. People have spread out blankets, runners and cyclists pass on the paths between the fields. When the sun sinks, the sky changes colour according to layers of pollutants, like dusty gold and orange and pink on an old canvas. And the next day, the heat increases. The heat is like oil, and I, a water bird, pointlessly wipe my nostrils, the corners of my mouth and my eyes with my fingers. Andrea dismisses as a fantasy my idea that the heat is poisonous, she enjoys the warmth. In the city, police cars drive through the streets in anticipation. There is murder and, more frequently, manslaughter. The children scream, not playing or arguing, but with rage. They're screaming at the world, my sister says.

In her flat, high on an upper floor, you can't hear the street noise, but on the other hand it's even hotter. My sister's child lies limply in her arms, feverish. When I was holding the little one just now, I could feel the infant's hot forehead through the fabric of my dress. My brother sits bent forward in an armchair, head lowered, elbows on knees. He leans backwards, tilts back his head, then resumes his previous position. He takes a deep breath and slowly exhales. Maybe you caught it from her. My sister gestures with her chin at the child in her arms and then at my brother. I go to him and lay a hand on his forehead. He flinches, your hand is awfully hot. So is your forehead. We're probably all feverish. My sister shifts her child from her right to her left arm, a damp patch of sweat remains on her right upper arm. What a heatwave, 30 degrees should be bearable. But it's unbearable. And yet, we're bearing it, my brother exhales. We bear a lot. I'm so tired. You aren't sleeping well either? No one is. Everyone talks of exhausting nights.

Through the open window, I constantly hear engines, honking, wailing, ambulance sirens. The flat is on the same street as the largest hospital in the city. I sit at my table, exhaustion pulls my arms down from my shoulders and presses against my skin from inside. I can feel the corners of my eyes, my lids, the fine musculature. There are no nerves in the eyeball, one's own gaze is a void of sensation. I raise my eyebrows, stretching the skin on my cheeks but my vision is still no clearer. A voice rises above the traffic noise, threatens murder, fucking, assault. I see people on the street looking around, it's impossible to tell whose voice it is; they hurry away. In the window above them, my burning eyelids, my swollen face.

Over the course of the day, the engine noise penetrates deeper into my body, the low rumble into my chest cavity, the roar under my skull at the back of my head, the wailing in through my ribs. In the evening, the light fades and the traffic grows lighter. I could call someone. I go out, walk through the streets, past restaurant terraces. How many people have called someone? I don't see anyone out alone, I don't catch anyone's eye before I'm back in my flat, standing at the window, the voids unchanged.

Andrea stood up and walked around the table. You can't say that. I look under her armpit at the table, she has put both arms around me. On the kitchen table is the cup from which I drank my early morning coffee with an ice cube. Not a single hour of the day brings relief. It's noon and Andrea's hands are on my back. My shirt is damp beneath them, her hands rub the damp fabric back and forth. Her mouth is at my ear, her voice and warm breath on the skin of my head. My pocket diary lies next to the coffee cup. I can't remember if my one appointment is scheduled for today or tomorrow. Andrea says she has to leave. No problem, I say. Better? I can see the nod she expects from me in the way she holds her head and I hug her so that we don't have to look at each other. You do mean well. She strokes my back one last time. As soon as she's gone, I'm going to put on a fresh shirt. I'm sorry. But what for? I change my shirt and look at my calendar, remember that the appointment was moved to next week. I swallow the coffee and the grounds in the cup. How's work going? Andrea had asked. For some time now, I've barely seen any of the dream figures, they're avoiding me. You have to get out more and see people.

It's evening again and I'm sitting on the floor in front of the open window. The heat is rising as the light weakens. A single siren outside, it's peaceful, it's Sunday. My hands lift vaguely from the wood floor, soon they'll be invisible. It doesn't matter if I'm there or not. You can't say that. I call Ulrich. It's so hot. I look at the night outside my window and then into the room. The objects on the table are indistinct. I know that my coffee cup from this morning is still there. You should get out of the city. I have to work. You can afford to take two days off, Ulrich says, I can too. I'll pick you up at nine tomorrow. I'll find a room. Two rooms. Sleep well. I get up, get my cigarettes, return to the window. I smoke two cigarettes then turn on the light. I look through the invoices lying on the table, fill a basket with dirty clothes, take them to the laundry room.

Such a lovely evening, Andrea says on the phone. We agree on a place to meet. How are you? I spent two days in the country with Ulrich. Andrea laughs. And how was it? It was really nice to see you, he said when we were saying goodbye and I only now realize that at some point during those two days I had talked about how women are fixated on assuring each other how nice it has been to be together. Insisting on how nice something was is sure to destroy it, I said and Ulrich laughed. Facing me, Andrea waits for me to tell her. I have a bad conscience. Really? I move my head. I listen. I don't remember what I said in response. I feel pity. I should have said, it was nice to see you too. Andrea's therapist thinks that for much too long we weren't nearly egoistic enough. I've had the feeling lately that something inside me has let go, Andrea says, that I'm no longer as dependent on how others see me. More ego. The good ego.

Hello! a woman said this morning when she suddenly appeared before me in the fruit shop. She smiled, she knew me. I took a step back and the friendliness drained from her expression. I had to clear my throat to say something, but I couldn't feel it. I saw her displeasure grow and watched her turn away to finish her purchases, glancing back repeatedly across the shop at the person I am. I picture her before me now, a line drawn with one stroke, nothing mended, nothing erased. I know her. But I have no idea where I'd met her before. A hole in my memory.

Do you really think a self-image is necessary in this world? You can't withdraw from it, Andrea says. I can't stand the traffic noise any more, I'm getting jittery from the sirens that rip me from sleep. It's much too loud. No wonder no one ever comes to see me.

Since her mother left, Andrea no longer drives out to see her father. He's lonely, tragically self-centred. He can't really see me, Andrea says, I have to protect myself. Sometimes she calls him and afterwards feels almost defeated. Miriam says that her girlfriend hates her own mother. At night, Miriam fears for her girlfriend's life. Lying next to her, she waits, sometimes a few minutes, sometimes an hour; she holds her breath until her girlfriend, twenty-one, twenty-two, twenty-three, twenty-four, twenty-five, twenty-six, twenty-seven, twenty-eight, takes another deep breath. Usually, it only takes ten seconds. Their nights together are sleepless ones for Miriam, but since they're so rare, she can bear it. Miriam is convinced that her girlfriend's sleep apnea is caused by her living situation. Her girlfriend's mother doesn't speak German and never goes out. Her only connection to the outside world is daily video calls with relatives on another continent. That's no way to live. Her girlfriend promised to find a doctor a year ago. Miriam says that her girlfriend's mother is probably severely depressed. It's impossible to imagine the pressure that comes from an immigrant background like that. Or the cultural differences.

How are you? Time passes so quickly. How can I manage more than just getting through the day? Laughter and, in the corners of their eyes, panic. I go to appointments, take on assignments, one social evening follows another. What project are you working on right now? I go outside with Ulrich for a cigarette. Before, you would have criticized them as do-gooders. He smiles. Today, he says, I think they're all afraid. Just wounded children.

My sleep keeps getting deeper and emptier. Sometimes I even try to sleep during the day to find the dream. You shouldn't do that. Dreams require certain behaviours and strict standards. Unhappy? I can't imagine how anyone can live without dreaming. Lately Andrea can't remember her dreams either, and her sleep, she says, has been unbelievably regenerating. The absence of any memory of dreams is a common misperception, what's necessary is to draw a connection. I seem to have been struck by night blindness; I can't find the door. Andrea says that not seeing a way out is a fundamental part of depression. Maybe there's just no place for dreams any more, I say. Andrea knows that, seen objectively, our world is a vale of tears, but still she finds it concerning that chemicals in the form of pills can change this perception within a few weeks. What a relief it is to let someone help you. It was her choice, her therapist told her, if she'd rather climb the mountain with or without a ten-kilo backpack. When coming to terms with your own past, there's no way around it, but you can make the process easier.

What about sadness and melancholy, anguish, apathy, Weltschmerz? Depression, Andrea says, means something other than not feeling anything as is generally assumed. I look at my forearm on the tabletop, in the sunlight the small round mark is visible. A dog barks in the flat next door, every day, nonstop. Is it being beaten? Left alone. It's a hopeless barking for company.

Only isolated sentences remain and even fewer that make any sense while in reality one word follows another as one sentence follows the next. Everyday a stream of talk. I have a vocabulary notebook, like the ones they used in language class. The foreign words in the left-hand column, the translation that makes them understandable in the right. In my vocabulary notebook, the right-hand column is empty on every page. To the left of the thin, pale-red lines, individual words are listed, one beneath the other, sometimes idiomatic expressions, half-sentences and whole ones.

The doctor who they claim performs miracles treated Miriam's brother who's a dreamer, she says. There's a long waiting list but, exceptionally, he gave me an appointment after hours. It will take nothing less than a miracle to find my dreams again. I take the express train to the other end of the city, to a neighbourhood that used to be outside the city limits. A storm has massed on the horizon. I imagine the miracle as a dreamcatcher with turquoise beads and brown-and-white speckled feathers. I had a dreamcatcher like that when I was little. Back then I had a natural rapport, as they say, with dreams.

When I get off the train, the rain has started to fall. I brace myself against the gusts of wind. The doctor who's meant to be a miracle worker has his office in an historic building, from the late Middle Ages, a stone staircase, a wrought-iron gate in front of every door. The gate and the door to the office are open, the reception room has a ribbed vaulted ceiling, the window, well above head-height, is dark, as is the screen on the receptionist's desk. The doctor invites me into the next room with a wide leather chair under another dark window with a wooden casement. I sit with my back to the wall and he sits with his back to the door, which he leaves open. Between us is a low table. What can I do for you? His smile doesn't falter for a moment. I look through the reception room at the closed front door and can't remember if he also closed the wrought-iron gate.

I can't work any more. What kind of work do you do? I write reports. What kind of reports? Reportage. A journalist, he says. Yes, I say. Not a secure job. I nod. Afraid for your livelihood? I don't know what else I could live on. He smiles. I'll write you a prescription, it works miracles. He takes a notebook and a fountain pen from his desk, writes quickly and with a flourish. He puts the pen down again, tears a page from the notebook. You're sceptical, a sign of intelligence. But your scepticism is unfounded. You'll see, it only helps you be yourself again. In California, where I trained, everyone's on it. He doesn't touch the two bills I laid on the desk. On the way out, I pass him in a movement that looks awkward. I'm now closer to the front door. He hands me the prescription, holds my hand firmly. Will you start it? Tomorrow, I say. Clever girl. I run. I told him that I had to catch the express and he replied, all the best. The storm pushes me along the street to the station.

Back in my flat, I place a large ashtray in the middle of the table. The handwritten prescription flared as it burned. I light a cigarette and smoke it slowly. I met the devil but didn't tell him anything about my dreams. I'm not saying you're crazy, Andrea says, but resisting help can be pathological.

I go out early at night, after all, they must be somewhere. Once in a while I do see one during the day, always on the other side of the street and always unexpectedly, a fleeting glance that snaps back a moment later only to find no one there. It's hard not to look for them. I want to wander aimlessly through the streets at night. Before, I also lived here, as I have in almost every part of town. A neighbourhood that looks shabby without being run-down, with plain buildings from after the war, without ornament, without eaves or windowsills. I find a particle-board door, like a temporary entrance, to a construction site, three steps above street level, ground-floor premises. An unplastered facade, boarded-up windows, unused, vacant. I pause on the second step, the door is ajar. They haven't locked me out. They're like children caught up in their game. It could be that they notice when I go, but without regret, and when I come back, they take me in because I enter their space. Brightness and movement through the crack in the door. The light from the streetlamps is weak, I can't lift my arm. No one is going to open the door for me. You have to take the first step.

I find a flat in the building with the particle-board door. I look for a tenant to replace me, terminate my old rental contract, sign the new one, pay what's owed, and finally move my table, chairs and mattress into the new flat. The particle board is replaced by a modern door of metal and glass, a sign indicates a mental health group practice.

My eyelids twitch, I turn my head to the side, he disappears in the corner of my eye. I let my head rest and don't try to open my eyes wider. The dream writing is smaller than my waking handwriting and tighter, lightly sloping to the left in order to cross over unnoticed.

He turns off the bedside lamp, rolls onto his side, straightens the covers, an actor simulating blissfully falling asleep. At 1.00, he takes a first, weak pill, at 2.00, a second. He doesn't turn on the light. A glass of water stands on the bedside table with the pills next to it. He goes to the toilet in the dark. Until 3.00 he is confident of his sense of time, after that his perception becomes detached from the clock. A half hour might feel like two or three hours or like five minutes. He has no sense of whether time is speeding up or slowing down. The stove in the kitchen shows the time in glowing blue numbers. At 2.30, he takes another weak pill and a half. None after 2.30, never more than five total. He keeps his eyes shut. The beams of the headlights sweep through the room on the other side of his eyelids.

The parquet floor is a pale expanse. My next step will show if it can bear weight. I'm standing on the threshold between the two rooms. In every flat I need two rooms, no matter how small, so that I can go from one into the other. The rooms in the new flat have high ceilings and high windows. One side looks over the street, the other over an inner courtyard shared by four buildings. I've never seen night-time illumination as bright as in this flat. The pale expanse could also be a reflection, a mirroring of the light absorbed from the room. The ceiling isn't visible. I put my foot on the wooden floorboards. A lack of noise is a sign, but in dreams it's hard to check something's reality. When awake, you may feel the need to grab something, to make sure; the question is what, then, are you holding? I stand at the window. In the courtyard, people go silently in and out of the buildings' back doors, some need to leave, others take their place. Names are murmured in the staircase, in the narrowest sections of the winding stairs, where you can't see. Who should be warned, who'll be taken next, who will escape with their lives?

At 3.00, he rolls onto his back and rests a hand on his lower belly. He concentrates on taking deeper breaths, past his throat and farther down. The distance from his upper chest to his diaphragm is too great for his breath. He tries, bit by bit, down to his lower ribs, from there outwards to his hand and his diaphragm does, in fact, lift but he lacks breath above it. He opens his mouth and gasps for air. Don't stand up, keep lying down, keep breathing. He doesn't always follow the rule of trying for two hours minimum.

He doesn't need any light, doesn't bump into any projections from the wall, door frames or table edges. Water is a strange element. In the darkness, he took a glass from the dish rack and twisted the faucet handle upward. He doesn't find any stream of water under it. One hand holds the glass, the other fumbles in the sink until it finds something that feels like cloth, smooth. He doesn't hear any noises from outside, only inside sounds, his breath, a tendon in his shoulder when he lifts his arm. First a car engine out on the street, the plug between his fingers, then the cold wetness on his ear and hand. His other hand, holding the glass, finds the stream of water. Ammunitioned is what he calls it when he has inserted the silicon earplugs and placed the plastic shield on his lower teeth.

My hands twitch, my leg muscles tense. I smell smoke and hear the crackling but can't determine which direction it's coming from. My only instinct is to rush off in a panic, anywhere at all. I see the trap the moment fangs pierce my neck. I gasp. Palpate my throat, the intact skin over my collarbones down to my ribs. I follow the knocking into the other room, which is empty except for a shape in the centre. A tree, covered with lichen, aerial roots. Approaching, I recognize behind the curtain a structure of bones, connected by cartilaginous joints, countless ramifications that spread away from the main trunk in ever-finer twigs. A coral colony, swaying gently in draughts of air or in currents of water, I don't know if we're above or below the parquet floor. A stronger movement, a flinch, a billowing, something flails deep in the branching coral with fins or wings. I've already stretched out my arm to reach inside, the reef is pale, the calcareous skeleton sharp.

At 4.30, he sits in the kitchen of his dark flat, a glowing square in his lap. He flinches, closes his eyes, opens them again before he can finally focus on another bright square, a window in the building across the way, that has so often signalled dawn. The fluorescent tubes flash on, flicker a few times before they shine consistently, a cold, white light, that doesn't leap out, doesn't spread, doesn't give off any warmth. The crackling doesn't come from flammable organic material, but from electric voltage, the soft hum is steady. He turns off the square in his lap, briefly rests his hand on it. Screen light can never be warm. There are artificial fireplaces, however, no one has managed to create realistic fake fire. Flames are unpredictable. In the building across the road, behind thin curtains, a shadowy figure stands in front of a wardrobe, getting dressed. He lies down for an hour or two.

Grinding is an aspect of parasomnias, the shield is meant to make the jaw relax. The friction of the teeth is irrelevant; all stone and all land will erode faster or slower depending on the strength of the forces. He's so tired that it seems enough just to stretch out on his back in bed, he'll surrender more completely, down to the ground and even deeper. Gravity's seat is in the centre of the earth, there you could probably rest. He hasn't yet reached the foundation of sleeplessness.

I stand at the open window before dawn, below is the old man who goes to the courtyard to smoke day and night. Not remembering your dreams only means that you've turned your back to them. I turn around and go to the table in the centre of the room. Now and then in the morning I find something written on the notebook on the floor near the mattress. In the dark, the letters leaned in different directions, the words flowed into each other. The coral reef, chlorine-bleached calcium. There are no nights as bright as day, the night's brightness is always different than the day's. The paper is also a pale expanse, on which I can effortlessly follow the movements of hand and pen. But it doesn't yield anything, the letters disappear immediately.

The tree with the thick drapery of lichen reaches forward. Spanish moss, a plant from the deep south, fairy hair on ancient swamp cypresses. Feeds on air, turns green only after it has rained. For the most part, the meshes of thicker and thinner shoots dangle from the trees, grey, similar in colour to the coral reefs that have repelled their algae and, after a time, starved.

You have to be kind to yourself. Obliging. You always perceive yourself from the outside as well. As a reflected person, you have no continuous identity. The thing with identity seems to keep getting more complicated. Or simpler. Lots of people suffered under the earlier, rigid concept of identity, someone says. More cognac is served. Terrible. I stop listening. Miriam nods, her eyes open wide. Since yesterday, pictures of the Mississippi Delta have been spreading around the world. She doesn't know which she finds worse, the many dead sea creatures or that children are dying on land from the toxic gas produced by the algae. Not to mention that hurricane season is coming. It makes you want to creep into a mouse hole. No, someone counters, you've got a political responsibility. I go out to smoke a cigarette. Only Andrea reacts, gestures that she'll join me, nods in response to a sign I give her and remains seated. I'd raised my hand to my ear. I pretended I was going to make a phone call.

Through empty streets with wide pavements lined with trees on the left and right, above me a dark-green roof. A carpet of aquatic plants, light and sounds are muffled, I barely hear my own steps or any stifled whispering. Next week I'll move into another flat. I find the figures in the staircase whispering, for their lives are unbearable. I'm always trying to catch names or maybe how someone could still be saved but can never understand any of the murmuring. Still, I know that none of them can be helped. I'll live in another part of the city; I've already signed the lease and given notice on the old flat—I've had practise in this. How can you stand it, Andrea asks from time to time. I can't stand it anywhere. I ask friends with a car to help me move my few pieces of furniture. I have to leave the coral branches behind; it will surface somewhere else. If the algae grow too thick on the water's surface, it becomes difficult to breathe below.

A sound, a murmur, a very soft whistle. A figure emerges from the shadows of a side street or a building entrance. Good evening. We walk side by side through the night, the air in this neighbourhood full of gardens and parks is cooler than in the city centre. Are you also coming from a party? From work. Do you know the observatory? He gestures to his right into the darkness. It's a dark night, unusually dark, heavily overcast with a new moon. All the way to my building's front door, we don't meet a single soul. Inside the flat, you can't see your hand in front of your face. A wall of flames, tall and short, wide, plump and twig-thin, flickering, falling on each other, collapsing into a single flame and rising again, then calm, perfectly straight, growing smaller. Embers glow inwardly. Are you asleep? A voice says something I can't understand. Are you there? Of course, I am. When I wake, it's daytime. The mattress, on the edge of which I'm sitting, the floorboards, on which my feet rest, on which the sunlight falls, through the curtainless window.

For several weeks I've been expecting a phone call, a complaint about the wall of fire in my old flat, then I realized that the flames have sunk into the masonry, that they're smouldering there in secret, or have spread to the next flat and jumped to one of the neighbouring buildings. If they emerge somewhere, no one will tell me. No one owns flames.

Remember how, when we were teenagers, we stubbed out burning cigarettes on our forearms? On the backs of our hands. Andrea raises her left hand. Bodily experiences, the skin as a border between the self and the world. The sea is too loud to hear our breathing, calm enough to talk. A bay in a small Spanish city, a birthday celebration that goes on for three days. Andrea talks about Janoš. I think he was my first love, she says. A winter scene, snow and the blue hour before darkness falls, but my memory is bathed in a warm light. I remember your feelings for him, I say. We're sitting next to each other on the damp sand, a crescent moon above the black water. The intensity of your first emotions, Andrea says, perhaps the purest of all. When you know nothing about anything. The waves are advancing, over the wooden planks we'd walked on earlier. Your whole life ahead of you, as they say. Next to the university building there were meadows, rare wetlands, are there any left?

At the time, we didn't think about the concept of eternity. The tides follow the moon as they always have, the sea is expanding, becoming even more violent, life in it keeps decreasing. I drink the last swallow from my beer bottle. If our vision extended far enough, we could see from here to the coast of Africa. I know what's going on out there. But now and then I have to think only of my little, personal life so I don't kill myself. I don't say anything. You're scaring me, Andrea says. I won't say any more, I promise. You think you're being objective, but your reality is not the truth. It's about my thoughts. I believe in positive energy and that it can make the world a better place, Andrea says. I'm cold. I have to protect myself from your negativity, Andrea says. I'm cold, I say and stand up. Brush the damp sand from my clothes. We go back without speaking.

It's the last evening, in a garden. I'm speaking to someone I used to know well. You haven't changed at all. We sit on a low wall off to the side. He's just finishing a long work about the German Romantics. Didn't we want to set off somewhere then, at least as far as Venice? Smiles. I want to know details about his work, he bends forward. And you? Wildfire. What? Bush fires, forest fires, I say, vegetation fires. There's no equivalent in German for wildfires. Although wildfire is a beautiful word, romantic. And you like that? I laugh. Sometimes I have an irrational fear of what's coming. It makes no sense. We're the last of our kind. My daughter won't miss what she's never known. You have a child and you only mention it now? It doesn't change anything, if you're unhappy or cheerful. And you have to admit it's an insult. You probably work too much and sleep too little. On the contrary, to me sleep is like morphine.

Fish and shellfish have become hard to find. Even sardines. One of the hosts has joined us. There's no poor man's food in that sense any more. A week ago, thousands of dead fish floated into the bay, most have been cleaned out by now. I say goodbye. You can't do that, the man I used to know well says, who knows when we'll see each other again in this life. I'm dead tired, you know. The morphine? He didn't miss a word. Do you tell your daughter fairy tales and legends? Unfortunately, she doesn't want to hear them any more. I put my glass down. I have to go, I'm drunk, I say, and they laugh. I raise my hand and wave goodbye.

The sea has advanced to within a few steps. I walk towards it. The water is as black as the sky, scattered reflections of light on the waves. A carpet of algae spreads out before me. Jellyfish swim in the deep water farther out off the coast. No one knows what kind they are or where they've come from and it's a mystery why the oxygen deficiency doesn't kill them. Lines of light appear in the water. A decision has been made to talk about poisonous jellyfish and the need to get rid of them. They know what's coming, they don't flee. Andrea sits beside my bed and touches my forearm with her fingertips, stroking my arm up to my shoulder and down to my wrist. Suddenly you were gone. Did you walk back alone?

Flames are the epitome of fleet-footedness, they rush without haste, they race over grasslands and up tree trunks, from treetop to treetop, over oil slicks, they literally drink gas. He walks with quick, light steps and often whistles as he goes. Not with his lips—his mouth is neither rounded nor pursed, you can't see his whistling, it comes from somewhere deeper. When he gets up in the night, goes to the toilet, to the kitchen for a glass of water, he doesn't walk as swiftly but still easily no matter how heavy his exhaustion. His exhaustion is often very heavy indeed and yet now and then his steps are completely silent. Sometimes his breathing is louder than his footsteps.

I trudge up the steep path against the wind, my arms braced at my sides, until I see the sign: Meteorological Institute. An historical building on a hill at the edge of town—it looks almost modest compared with the villas around it. The lawn behind it slopes gently downwards and on it are various measuring instruments and a tower that is more a scaffold, a tall steel structure consisting only of stairs and a platform. The oldest instruments are set up on the roof of the main building, on a turret that one climbs like the highest lookout on a fortress. There's no view from the room in which he works. When he glances from the screen to his desk, he sees an old plane tree and the windowless wall of the building on the adjacent property.

I bring the mattress, the table and the chairs with me. Ulrich makes three trips in his car, then it's done. My new flat has only one room and a kitchen nook but there is a doorsill between them I can cross back and forth. There's space for a mattress, table and chairs; the room looks over a back courtyard, to which there's only one door and which is empty, no frame for beating carpets, no dustbin, no bike rack. A moss-covered strip of ground. No street noise, no sirens, the building is not more than fifty years old. What are you working on now? Ulrich asks. Enormous toxic algae blooms along the coasts of Florida, Turkey and southern Europe, the dramatic extinction of coral reefs not only in Australia but also in Polynesia—mass fish die-offs. The acidification of the Mississippi Delta. Swamp cypresses that are hundreds of years old and can grow to be a thousand are suffocating. You know what dead zones are? Ulrich says, this is unbearable. Yes, it's unbearable. You never say anything about yourself. That's not true. Yes, it is. I don't even know if you're in a relationship or not.

By early evening I'm already feeling heavy and ready to give in to sleep, to close my eyes, hopefully sleep will come quickly. In the morning, pain from my spine drills into the back of my head the way a shaft is driven into a mountain. Or around noon, when pushing open a door, there's a strain across my chest, too much lactic acid in my muscles, then I feel my lower back too. Sometimes I can attribute the physical traces to a memory, often they remain baffling.

He comes back from the burning fields with his skin dried out, his eyes inflamed. We look at each other the way you look at someone coming back from abroad, from a long journey, trying to read from their eyes, skin, posture, expression the experiences that might have changed them. My feet hurt with every step. On his cheeks I find hot, scaly spots. Once my lower lip split open, a small crack in the centre. I apply the salve he gives me. It works particularly well on burns but is meant for any wound.

What's that supposed to mean—he doesn't sleep? Andrea looks at me. He can't sleep? That sounds like a lack of ability, like not knowing how to swim or spell. He suffers from sleeplessness? Yes, sometimes he does, but it would be more accurate to say that he doesn't sleep. Not at all? That's not possible, Andrea says, you can't survive without sleep. How long has he had this condition? At least as long as I've known him. The longer sleep disorders last, the harder they are to treat. He has to do something about it. He's seeing a sleep therapist. Andrea says, stress is the main cause of insomnia. How do you know these things? She asks what kind of a job he has. I don't know anything at all, she says, you tell me so little. It's true, I'm finding it harder and harder to tell anything. In a prior life he was a fire lookout. What's that? He monitors forest fires. He's a scientist? He's one of those people who are obsessed with their field. At the university? He has a position at the Meteorological Institute, half of his salary is paid by the Academy of Sciences. What is his subject called? In most cases, he knows where a fire will start, he can tell from the way they behave. When he exhales, he sings softly. Is he a postdoc or a PhD? I really don't know.

The profession of fire lookout doesn't exist any more, today there are technologies and human assistants. But humans are still essential for last-minute forecasts, those that are so last minute that there's hardly any fore at all, an hour, a few minutes. *Nowcasts*. He uses English technical terms like foreign words, most of them mean nothing to him. He has never used the German term, the old one that is inextricably bound to meteorology. He talks about prognoses, calculations or estimates. He can't and won't predict anything. He says he's superstitious.

Does she schedule 'meetings' with her patients so they don't have to feel like patients? He looks at her, she looks at him. He compliments her on the term 'sleep coach', a trademark registered in her name. He calls her consultant. Her reserved smile. The sleep diary is the only suggestion he takes immediately. Still, he prefers to call it a log.

It's official, my sister says, a respiratory illness that has only recently been known and only affects children. The doctors don't know how to treat it. The illness spreads in kindergartens and elementary schools. The children become a little like old people. They move slowly. Not enough air to scream. My sister makes chest compresses for her child, every hour, all night long. She remembered our mother's stories about her mother's household remedies.

The consultant has charts with columns in which her patients enter what time they went to bed and when they got up, how long they slept. He creates his own document with a statistics programme on his computer. He understood right away that it was about gathering material, exposing connections he'd been unaware of. Diet plays a role. For a week or two he enters what he eats and drinks. Beef, salad, bread and cheese, four beers, goulash, wine, plum brandy, coconut cookies. What about environmental influences? Whatever seems important to you.

Next to the date, he notes the weather, indicates the temperature, humidity, wind conditions, cloudiness. He uses data from the nearest available weather station, usually the one at the Meteorological Institute and, therefore, also each station's location, latitude and longitude. Beneath each line, for each day, an assessment of sleep quality, a check somewhere between zero for very bad and ten for very good. He'd heard that you should not be judgemental in therapeutic contexts. But he came to her because he isn't sleeping well, didn't he? Because he can't sleep. There's no good or bad weather. There are conditions that are beneficial and those that are harmful.

In the last column he enters the sleep duration (SD) every day. It is the total time he presumably slept, which he sometimes estimates more generously, sometimes less, sometimes he includes dozing, sometimes he doesn't. Remember, the consultant tells him, four-and-a-half hours is enough to survive. She's always coming back to the principles of sleep hygiene. Regularity, a consistent rhythm, always get up at the same time, regardless of how the night went. Don't eat, watch television or work in bed and no artificial light. No screens less than two hours before going to bed. The detailed observation of sleep distribution is important, he calls it night quality: everything that happens between the time he goes to bed (BT) and the time he gets up (U), text boxes that only open when you click on them.

Sometimes I can't remember what I've already told you. I forget a lot. Well, the consultant says, I know that your profession is very important to you. After all these years, almost all my clients have only one common denominator: perfectionism and a pronounced sense of responsibility. They often have very demanding jobs. How late do you usually work? Until 18.00 or 19.00. Do you sometimes stay late? Sometimes. And do you work at home, at night, when you can't sleep? After a brief hesitation he says, occasionally. The consultant nods, that's what she thought. May I ask what exactly it is you do? I study forest fires. The consultant didn't know that it's part of meteorology. They're connected. Forests and the climate influence each other, without meteorology, you can't estimate the risk of fire. But he actually comes from outside. He isn't really part of the institute, he says. His office is behind the weather-forecast rooms at the end of the hall. In any case, he should try to avoid working at night. After all, the fires will burn whether you're asleep or awake, won't they?

The doctor prescribes the weak pills (PLS) with a smile as if he didn't take the medicine or the patient quite seriously. Maybe the weak pills hadn't worked or they no longer do. After taking the weak pills, he can fall into a doze one time out of five. That's enough for him to take them. A probability of one out of four doesn't mean that on the fifth night he'll sleep or just doze. Ten nights can pass without any sleep (S) or even dozing (D). The doctor orders stronger pills.

Worse than not sleeping is having to watch his muscles shut down while his brain keeps spinning. To feel all of his muscles relax whether he wants them to or not. His rear end releases first, his buttocks, which he didn't even realize he'd been tensing, suddenly the bones beneath them feel very pointed. His calves and thighs, it's not unpleasant. Then comes the relaxation of his chest and lungs. His diaphragm releases, his muscles along his ribs become soft, slide from his sternum down over his ribcage. He lies there with an open chest cavity. In it hangs his heart muscle, which doesn't yet yield. It contracts and expands as the wind sings in the structure and his lungs tremble.

But my thoughts haven't stopped, my head hasn't slept. The doctor no longer smiles. He says, you must have an unusually strong brain. Let's try something else. The doctor writes a prescription and says, these are guaranteed to work. Take two of them, don't ever take more. There are the weak pills (PLS) and the ones that are guaranteed to work (P).

The vibrations are transferred from the earth into the pole that is stuck in it and up to the head that is fastened to the pole, the centre in which the tension is concentrated. The black bristles and the grin on the head tremble. I hold the head in my hands. It's a walnut rattling in its shell, I weigh the fruit in one of the halves, a wrinkled face. He doesn't sigh, groan or wheeze. Beneath his eyelids, no movement is visible. He is silent and still. I hold my hand over his mouth, below his nose. His eyes snap open at the same time as his mouth to gasp for air. He struggles and, before he recognizes me, he must think for a moment that I'm the creature who has been sitting on his chest and squeezing his throat. That's pill-induced sleep.

Sometimes I want him to touch me so badly it hurts. I sit there, reading, Andrea says, while he walks around, busy with something, or I work, but actually I have no idea what I'm doing. I desperately wish I could be so absorbed in something that I don't notice him at all until he brushes me in passing, comes up behind me and puts his hands on my shoulders. I wonder if there's any greater loneliness than that of a child who is supposed to be sleeping but is wide awake behind closed eyelids. I pretended to fall out of bed in my sleep so that my mother or father would come to pick me up and lay me back in bed, would sit next to me until I fell asleep. Mostly no one noticed me and I snuck back into bed. I want him to touch me so badly it hurts. Why don't you go to him? To hurt him?

A black mask is fastened around his head. Beneath it, his breath, a trickle, the tighter the mask, the thinner the trickle. A slender stream, nose and mouth and trachea aligned, a black line. Breathing in and out through this line to keep from disappearing. The barely audible whistle. Are you asthmatic? the consultant asks. There are causes that trigger inflammation, that's what they say. Are you getting treatment? I'm sitting here. From a specialist who knows the condition, she says and looks at his chest then again at his face. I have an inhaler, as needed, he says. The consultant takes a deep breath and he is relieved because she can't always completely control herself. Because I'm a sleep expert I happen to know that sleep disorders can certainly be connected to asthma, she says. The symptoms often appear at night and in the early morning hours. Stress can exacerbate or relieve them. How do people die when they die of sleeplessness? People don't simply die of insomnia, as you imagine it. You know there's such a thing as fatal insomnia, he says. You know that's very rare condition which you don't have, the consultant replies. You're suffering from something else.

His head on the pillow, body on the mattress, slatted frame, third storey, five metres above the ground, bottomless exhaustion. He found a sleep mask from a trip he can't remember taking, from another time, with an airline logo. 2 PLS. He turns off the light, sits upright with his back against the wall for a moment, turns the light back on. 3 PLS. 5 PLS yesterday. The mask covers the upper half of his face, fits more snugly on the bridge of his nose. Hearing signifies the process through which waves from outside the body pass through the outer ear, into the inner ear, through the tympanic membrane, ossicles, hammer and cavity, and are turned into acoustic stimuli. The roar of your own blood is not a sound, it makes tangible the pressure on the vessels and the entire body. Ear plugs enhance the perception of your own pulse. The isolation doesn't help him sleep any better, but he takes these precautions to prevent being woken.

First, he turns his head away as if he could escape in one direction or the other, but the pressure builds, rises and falls, then collapses. He has raised his hands to his ears. A dark roar that withdraws and approaches, ever closer and ever louder. The tiny silicon plugs in his ear canals like a dam, like boulders against which a wave pounds, powerful and constant. His blood pumps, his tympanic membranes sway with the impact, still the boulders hold. He holds his fingers to his ears. The droning grows louder, even stronger than before, unbearable. With a quick motion, he'll remove both boulders at once. His eardrums will burst, the roar will stop. He'll lie quietly as his blood flows.

A torrent between two mountain slopes, grey boulders and scree, an area that never burns. Voices from somewhere, sentence fragments, a sound, my voice and others, unfamiliar, a groan, a cry. He has slept and was convinced he wasn't sleeping. The night is sticky, sheet lightning passes over his hot forehead. He doesn't open his eyes, he knows it's in the east. A flash from hairline to eyebrows, a second on his temples, a third strikes from the bridge of his nose to the centre of his forehead. I see the damage the following day.

Did you not sleep? Faced with his furrowed brow, swollen eyelids and inflamed eyes, I'm ashamed of my question. The storm hit east of the city. Barns burned, stalls filled with cattle, a farmer killed by a beam, trees uprooted. A bruise on his right wrist, another on his forearm. I look at his ribcage. When I can see him breathe but don't hear him, it's better. He waits for my glance. I look at his right eye. You need both eyes to see something as fully as possible. Looking into each other's eyes isn't possible.

I leaned out the window under a dazzling sky, I briefly saw the street and a car, not a sound, then it was dark again and between the walls, a pressure wave came at me. I pulled my head in at the last moment, back into the flat, where I heard the boom and stretched out flat on the floor. They have no idea what they're doing. Impeding heavy rain. How can a meteorologist believe he can control the atmosphere?

Now and then he reads through his notes when he enters the night's data, lying on the couch, the glowing rectangle propped against his bent legs. He aimlessly scans the rows and columns, indifferent to the significance of the numbers and letters. The steadily increasing quantity of data has a calming effect, often followed by a D, sometimes a few Ss. S means proper sleep. A few times he was tempted to suggest to the consultant that she use the log as a bedtime story but refrained to keep from drawing her attention to his notes. What do you consider good sleep? she'd asked him. You know what sleep is when you've had it. If you think about it later, it wasn't real sleep.

Eyes glowing like coals, red and black, I wonder if the consultant finds him as beautiful as I do. Tell me what's good in your life? My life, he says. Do you divide your life into good and evil? She finds it notable that he contrasts the good with the evil and not the bad. He finds that believing in evil is more tolerable than accepting the bad. A misconception he wants to hold on to. Good in my life. What I mean, she said, is in what moments, with whom do you feel happy, safe, warm? He winces, nods, thinks it over. Please give me an example, he says, what would you say if I asked you what's good in your life? I'd say my grandchildren. You have grandchildren? He's surprised and notices the effort she makes not to feel flattered. You didn't hesitate. It's simple, she replies

The consultant suggested they meditate together. After the second time he said that he didn't know much about meditation but was wondering if this didn't make a mockery of Buddhist and Hindu traditions. Then she spoke of mindfulness exercises and after a while only of exercises, which he found most fitting. The treatment room is a large space that feels small and narrow with floor-to-ceiling bookshelves that seem to be overflowing on one wall. Now and then they eject one or two books which then lie on the floor. On the far wall, a plant has begun to grow horizontally over the window. On the desk, at which he's never seen the consultant sit, are stacks of paper, on the ground there are single pages that one draught of air wafts here and there, while another lifts them, rustling, from time to time. The floor is covered with overlapping rugs strengthening the impression that the room is in constant motion and the woman in it is an earth scientist, insignificant among the microscopic and tremendous upheavals. The black couch, on which he takes a seat, a low glass table, and across from them, the consultant's leather armchair. He'd made enquiries. Actually, you're a psychotherapist. Smile. What difference does that make?

She unrolls two mats in the only available space, one in front of the bookshelves, the other in front of the desk, sweeping away several papers with a practised motion. He stretches out on the mat in front of the bookshelf, the consultant lies down on the other. There are recordings of her calming voice for sale. He looks at the stucco decorations on the ceiling and wonders what the consultant is thinking when she says these sentences, which she could recite in her sleep. At this thought, he laughs softly. Hears the tiny pause in her speech but she doesn't ask. Feel your ribcage fill with air. Let the air stream into your belly your diaphragm rise and sink, your breath stream in and out.

When he lies on the mat waiting for the bookshelf to throw a book on him and for the consultant to speak her sentences with pauses to give him time to feel, he does actually feel sleepy now and again. Don't try to control your breath, it will happen on its own. Let go. He doesn't tell the consultant that he doesn't know how breath streams. He's too used to the sounds and the feeling of constriction in the various areas, in his throat, below the top of his sternum, in his bronchial tubes and his lungs, too used to hearing the high, polyphonic whistling and the droning to be able to connect his breath and his belly.

Andrea is afraid that her fear will return. She thought she'd mastered it once and for all. But for some time now, I've felt it again, only occasionally and not for long, then suddenly a gloom spreads over everything and that taste in my mouth, bitter and sharp. What is it you see? War. You can't deny it. This overpowering, panicked fear, Andrea says, is not a normal reaction. It has something to do with me, they're repressed emotions. She says that the causes lie deep in her childhood.

In the worst attacks, abdominal cramps set in. It's the cramps he fears, the faint whistling doesn't bother him, it sounds like it's coming from very far away, as if his lungs were vast. Imagine there's a light in your stomach, the consultant says. Put a hand on your belly if you want, just below your navel. Feel the warmth emanating from the light in your stomach. He doesn't need his hand to imagine a light; light is fire. An underground fire, gas burns and draws oxygen from the surface through a pipe. He finally does lay his hand on his stomach. The warmth travels through his muscles and fatty tissues and skin and reaches his hand.

The consultant occasionally asks if he does the exercises at home. The one with fire in my stomach, he says. The light, you mean. The exercise with the light in my stomach. She asks if it helps him sleep through the night. He replies that he doesn't know what sleeping through means. The consultant nods. Do therapists need to experience successes? I do my work to help people. People come to me because they want to change something, and I support them. You once told me that I could modify all the exercises, he says. You know best exactly what it is you need, the consultant replies.

Did you know that fewer weather advisories are given during the night? There's no objective reason for this, weather stations are staffed around the clock. It's not due to the weather, it's due to caution. There's no greater watchfulness than that of parents guarding their child's sleep. Those who sleep don't contend. They entrust themselves to their guardians.

Worst of all, the consultant says, is the light from screens. Worst of all are memory lapses. Sleeplessness breeds moths inside your skull, behind your forehead. They lay their larvae in the most hidden folds, in the deepest layers and then the larvae feed on your brain mass. They don't differentiate, they eat indiscriminately, so that one day you develop a scotoma, you don't see a step, you stumble or treat someone you should know like a stranger. There are blinds spots of all kinds. Cells are renewed, they take over different areas, the brain adapts and learns, but memory cannot be replaced. New impressions are stored in memory, but the past is irretrievably lost. This can persist undetected for a long time until one day, by chance, it comes to light.

Do you remember, someone asks and you realize that you don't. You examine the source of the memories and find yourself looking through patchy, gnawed-out holes at empty hands. He wonders if the consultant knows that moths shun light. You're wrong, I say, they're drawn to artificial light and seek out dark corners to lay their eggs. My brain full of larval eggs. The connection between sleep disorders and Alzheimer's has been statistically established. The consultant insists he shouldn't turn the light on at all at night, not even to get a glass of water. Light interrupts the production of melatonin, every second of light after you go to sleep, she says. After you go to bed, he says. Before, older people only talked about lying down. No artificial light, the consultant constantly returns to the rules of sleep hygiene. Revolting, I say. He takes a cigarette from the pack between us on the mattress. We listen to music, he rolls the cigarette between his fingers, puts it down, picks it up, then finally lights it and hands it to me.

People no longer tend fires; they have no space for them. They often know nothing about fire, they don't know about combustion even though they cause it with every push of their finger. Absolute rule always ends disastrously. What's your name, someone asks, and the other one says, I am. Most names are useless, arbitrary or treacherous. He's the scion of fruit farmers, the first and last born, the one on whom they've pinned their hopes. The trees—apple, cherry and sour cherry—were their pride and their capital. The trees could no longer survive where he was born and after he left, neither could his parents.

The consultant asks about sleep disorders in the family, she wants to explore his biographical background. There's such a thing as learnt sleep behaviour. What kind of rituals did your parents have, was there a common bedtime? That has all become fodder for the moths. The destruction of an orchard can take a very long time. Each year is considered a bad one until it eventually becomes clear that there won't be any more good years. There are still healthy trees there, even if flies nest in the cherry-tree leaves one year and the next year beetles bore under the apple-tree bark, making them die of a thirst for which there is no remedy.

The year after that, an unknown rot creeps into the fruits' core, into the stem, into the pit. They have to cut down more and more trees and each year they discover more black patches and white spots, they prune withered branches, and hope something will grow back. The spaces between the remaining trees grow larger and even the seedlings in the greenhouse don't stand a chance. The torment of wanting to keep something alive under the most adverse circumstances and the despair when it's futile.

Do you have any siblings? No siblings. When did you leave home? When it was over. After your parents' death? There was nothing left. In fact, it's never about sleep. Insomnia points to a problem that must be solved. Only in mathematics are there problems that can be solved.

Why won't you show him to us? Andrea asks. What do you think we'll do to him? Miriam laughs. For once, she has brought her girlfriend, for an hour, then her girlfriend has to work the night shift. She seems completely normal, very nice, Andrea says, and I could see that Andrea has to make as much of an effort as I do not to look at Miriam's girlfriend's mouth and throat and chest, to see how she breathes. After she leaves, Miriam says that her girlfriend's mother is convinced she's suffering from early stage stomach cancer. So she's drawing her daughter even closer. Andrea nods. She asks if I'm hiding him or if he's the one hiding. I want to keep him for myself. Andrea says, I'm not sure he's good for you. Miriam smiles.

As a child I learnt that mumps are a big lump in the throat that makes it hard to talk. Back then I was amazed that the mirror showed no large bulge, a swelling that now, after I've accumulated so many words, must be even more monstrous. The sensation in my throat is strange as long as I remain silent; only when I try to talk do I feel like gagging. How are you feeling? Talk as little and sleep as much as you can is what my mother said to the child with mumps.

Sometimes I turn the dishwasher on for him. There's a lot of furniture in his flat, as well as a fully furnished kitchen. I say, I'll cook properly today and dirty as many dishes as possible. He leaves me alone in the kitchen and if he thinks that the modest meal isn't in proportion to the effort it took to prepare it, he doesn't let it show. Late in the evening, he lies on the couch. At some point, a moth larva will be born in the memory of sleep and will feed on it. When I no longer remember what it was like to sleep, he says, then the grief will also be gone. I go to the kitchen and load the pots and pans, plates and glasses and cutlery into the dishwasher. It's an old appliance that consumes a lot of energy and makes a lot of noise. I turn it on, wipe the table, walk around the flat, still have things to do in the bathroom, while he lies on the couch and no more sound comes from outside, the room is full of whirring and surging and clicking. I brush my hand along his body, he turns his face to me with his eyes closed. Again, I walk through the rhythmic sound of the machine and the water into the next room and by the time I return he has fallen asleep. I drop into an armchair across from him, the whirring envelops us.

No one complains about too little sleep after a nice night. The consultant smiles. It's not the sleep deprivation per se. It's the quality of the sleep deprivation, he says. You could change the sleep quality scale into one that evaluates the sleep deprivation quality. The consultant has become serious again. It's a matter of what thoughts prevent you from sleeping, of what you want to avoid. Insomnia also is a matter of control. You're acting as if I don't want to sleep. The consultant looks at him expectantly. But I'm sitting here, I've been coming to you for how many weeks or months or years and there's been no improvement. I can show you my notes. One night last week I slept for six hours and you're still holding on to your dubious formula of four-and-a-half hours, of which I'm the living proof to the contrary. Sometimes more alive, sometimes less.

What do you even look like? Andrea's eyes sweep down my face, from my eyes over my mouth to my neck. Nights are exhausting. Have you stopped sleeping too? I dream a lot, twice as much as before. How often do you see him? I see him most of the time. She says, I have a feeling you're losing yourself. I ask her what she means. I think you identify too much with him. Is that bad? I can't believe you said that. You have to remain yourself. You should never give yourself up. I thought you saw things the same way, Andrea says. I really don't know what that's supposed to mean. A lot of words I don't understand, I say, the more I hear them, the less I understand them. I think you need to set better boundaries, she says.

how are you, I've left Ulrich, phone calls, messages, texts, emails, detachment, futility, boredom, habituation, therapist, relationship, projects, messages, texts, emails, individual, goals, messages, messages, how are you, yourself, dark, shadows, figures, hunched, caves, graphite, connection, computer, messages, texts, emails, how are you, good, yourself, conscience, how are you, toxic, positive, take pleasure, murder, fuck, smash, you can't say that, do well, mean well, do good, regret, feel, how are you, messages, texts, emails, yourself, feel, egotistic, have, feeling, therapist, perception, ego, self-image, see, protect, bond, relationship, depressive, migrant background, cultural differences, you can't say that, how are you, fear, hurt, bond, project, messages, texts, emails, depression, self, objective, understand, perception, psychological, accept help, conscious, therapist, past, sadness, melancholy, anguish, apathy, world-weariness, depression, how are you, messages, texts, emails, yourself, project, signify, feel, understand, alone, society, talk, words, understandable, depression, wonder, conditions, fears, live, yourself, myself, oneself, love, crazy, resistance, pathological, mental, healthy, psychological, conscious, self-conscious, fight for your life, help, psychological, conscious, become conscious of, make conscious of, feel, feel, I have the feeling, how are you, I believe, messages, texts, emails, self, relationship, project, oneself, oneself, oneself, accommodated, reflected, upon oneself, by oneself, to oneself, feel, identity, concept, feeling, how are you, self-perception, external perception, feel, dynamic, position, feeling, how are you, life, conscious, personal, murder, psychological, fear, reality, truth, objective, positive, energy, negativity, feeling, messages, texts, emails, you can't say, support, conscious, self, yourself, oneself, talk, eternity, meaningless, feel, believe, depression, support, meaning, disorder, unhappy, feeling, cheerful, dead, dead tired, alone, endure, unendurable, how are you, project, relationship, survive, stress, recount, session, dates, esteem, feel, feeling, really, self, feeling, how are you, reality, loneliness, stress, suffering, trigger, look in the eye, happy, safe, warm, self-worth, let go, conscious, stream, messages, texts, emails, fear, fear, fear, feel, fear, message, self, repressed feelings, intuitive, problem, how are you, quality, therapist, success, support, needs, own, self, own, hello, how are you, oneself, oneself, oneself, energy, relationship, information, disorder, problem, solution, talk, words, how are you, depression, project, yourself, oneself, you understand, I believe, identify with, talk, smile, believe, say, feel, function, oneself, yourself, believe, feel, talk, smile, feel, signify, you understand, give up, signify, understand, set boundaries

There are units of measurement for all the columns—hours, minutes, arc seconds, degrees Celsius, metre, kilometres per hour, millimetre, per cent, hectopascals, north, northeast, east, southeast, south, southwest, west, northwest—only in the text boxes does he work with data that can't be systematized. The text boxes can't be evaluated statistically. The only relation to be evaluated is the one between sleep duration (SD) as an effect and the frequency distribution of the respective variables. Therefore, in order to account for the influencing factor of a night's quality, he has established a limited number of possibilities. The NQ column contains long lists of the respective abbreviations.

ES stands for emergency sleep, PS for pill-induced sleep, meaning the pills that are guaranteed to work (P). He records the weak pills in the nutrition column (N), in which he doesn't record anything else. Food and drink could only be evaluated if it were categorized by group, but he assumes their influence is irrelevant. Another variable that he has simplified for the sake of evaluation is the ingestion of PLS. In the beginning he had precisely recorded what doses he'd taken at what time, but he simply now enters the total quantity under N, such that, for example, 2 indicates the one-time consumption of two pills, while 3 ½ div. signifies that over the course of the night a total of 3 ½ were ingested in at least two doses. Most often there is a D in the NQ column for dozing. D is not real sleep, but lying with a calm sequence of thoughts that occasionally stray and might bring him on the edge of real sleep. D allows a minimal level of recuperation.

When there is great despair, sometimes emergency sleep comes even without PLS or P in the early morning hours when he's sure that his organism wouldn't survive in the element of day. Sunlight would be unbearable for his eyes and skin, his hearing and lungs would collapse as soon as he entered day-to-day business on the street, just as the gas-filled cavities in the body are unable to adapt to too sudden and too large changes in pressure. On such nights, he breaks one of the most important rules of sleeplessness: Do not think of the coming day.

There are nights when the pain in his limbs is so great, his eyelids are so swollen, his eyes burn so much and each breath takes such an effort that discipline falls away. He begins to imagine how he'll get out of bed the next day and go into the bathroom, brush his teeth, wash his hair and then eat breakfast. He pictures himself going to work. He has to imagine each step, because each step takes an unimaginable effort. He has to move his legs, place his feet, lift them again, keep his eyes open, look around to see if anyone is coming at him, if the light is green, if the car is stopped. He can't lift his arm in front of his face. He hasn't even made it to work yet. He lies on his back, hands crossed on his chest, as if laid out in a coffin, he doesn't want anything any more. The mercy of emergency sleep, a short, restless loss of consciousness. It can't be relied on. Just because he's convinced his distress has never been greater, doesn't mean that emergency sleep will come.

What fascinates him is that it doesn't end. In the morning, he needs fifteen minutes to prop himself up and scoot to the edge of the bed where he remains sitting, the floor under his feet, the mattress under his hands, his head drooping, and sometimes it takes him another quarter of an hour to stand up. For an hour or more, he can't even think, exhaustion tugs at every fibre of his body from his neck muscles to his Achilles tendons. His only thought is that sleeplessness has made him stupid. Lifting his hand is an indescribable strain, brewing tea a series of exertions. Inhale. Inhale again. Exhale slowly. Breathe out more air. Breathe in again. What fascinates him is that two hours after getting up, he is actually going to work, talking with people who think of him as one of them, and occasionally he even forgets that he hadn't slept and how hard it was to get up.

It can all be traced back to the laws of energy. Energy can't be lost. Death, as it is generally understood, does not exist. The sleepless feel the energy of life in its entirety. Its mining works, on which he rests, everything he has. Every morning, the need to find an untapped vein from which to draw enough for the day. In metallurgy, exhausted means that only waste rock remains. Waste rock is material that serves no purpose. Dead rock was once living, like coral reefs. The question remains: What do you die of when you die of not sleeping? As does the doctrine of four-and-a-half hours.

What if I spend four-and-a-half hours dreaming that I'm awake, is that enough to survive? If I think about not being able to fall asleep while I am asleep, which according to you is truly shattering, do those four-and-a-half hours count as sleep or not? Do those four-and-a-half hours count as survival time? Sleeping and not sleeping, half–half? I did not say shattering. I could have sworn you said shattering. The consultant shakes her head. But we do agree that sleeplessness is shattering, right? You must know better than anyone; every day you've got I don't know how many abnormal sleepers sitting here. The consultant starts to say something. Which word, he interrupts her, would you use instead of shattering? Please don't say challenging. The consultant props her chin on her hand, which covers her mouth. To experience sleeplessness while sleeping is hell. She takes her hand away from her mouth. We don't need another word. Thank you. Assessing the relationship between insomnia and one's lifespan is an impossible statistical venture. To add up the hours of insomnia and subtract them from the average lifespan would be a naive delusion. The devil doesn't calculate that way.

He knows the statistics. Few people dare to draw a direct connection between sleep disorders and life expectancy. But it doesn't take much expertise to derive a significantly shorter life expectancy from the many studies of correlation between sleep disorders and various illnesses from heart disease and diabetes to dementia. Two studies establish a fivefold increase in risk of suicide. A Finnish study of twins estimates a roughly twenty-five per cent higher risk of early death on less than seven hours a night. How can you say someone has died before their time? As if we understood anything about the laws of space and time. You won't die, the consultant says. He looks at her, sees the thoughts surface on her face. Not for the time being, she says and lowers her chin in acknowledgment of the fact that one shouldn't say weighty things lightly.

You've turned me into an accountant, he says. Every day he estimates the prob. sleep duration, every week he makes a rough calculation meant to determine whether he will live or die, though without knowing exactly what he needs four-and-a-half hours of or within what timeframe it's necessary for survival. He has reviewed his entries from the previous two weeks. A total of eight hours, never more than two in a row, most of them D, not a single S. There are sleep labs or portable devices to use at home for a realistic assessment of his sleep time. In a lab, they'll measure all of the parameters, the consultant says. You'll be given a file with calculations from your total sleep time and waking hours, along with sleep latency, to waking frequency.

For the time being, the consultant doesn't deem an objective assessment of his sleep quality and quantity to be necessary. I think your own entries are more interesting, she says. You're still keeping a sleep diary? No sleep diary. You don't like my words, but doesn't it come down to the same thing if we call it a diary or a log? It's important to be precise, he says. The consultant brings up the concept of misconception. They're both used to English technical terms, which allows for interaction on equal footing. It's only logical, he says, that someone with sleep disorders also has disordered perception. At a certain level of sleep deprivation, visions and hallucinations set in.

In the alphabetized list of acronyms attached to the document for data entry, there is BMR—brain-machine rage. One of the abbreviations before prob. is dspr – despr. He doesn't want to write the word out in the list of acronyms either. As he quickly scans the collected data, the connection between dspr and PS is evident after just a few pages, even if he weren't looking for a correlation. The premises are constituted so that the programme can analyse the data and produce a report, for now he limits it to the continued collection of data. He hasn't set any limit to the period of assessment, which is necessarily finite.

Under a white sky, I walked through a blazingly bright city, clean and well-ordered, streets and squares paved with black asphalt, not a breath of air, not a leaf moved because there were no trees. I walked until I found a mess of scraggly, leafless shrubs in beds of dry earth. A flagstone path that I followed along a wide river with cargo barges. I took one of them to the sea. I wandered around the port, no one could give me any information. The salty wind grated against my forehead and cheeks, crystals burned on the tip of my tongue. To set the rain forest in Sumatra on fire, it first has to be dried out. Peat burns very slowly and for a very long time. No fires would start on their own here and none releases more pollutants from the old carbon-laden ground than this kind. Thick, black smoke, you don't see many flames. He coughs, inhales slowly and exhales with difficulty. The trees in the Sumatra jungle burn to their heartwood. If you wanted to indicate the destruction of life in levels, this would be the highest level, death to the very core.

I rub my aching feet. His eyes are bloodshot, and his slight coughs are dry. He tries to keep them from turning into coughing fits, which are hard to stop. The skin on his cheeks is tight. I go to the kitchen, fill the water pitcher and set it back on the table. It's not just my feet that hurt, my calves burn with every step. For some nights the entry reads DES—for desertification. He rubs his eyes, leaving black dust in the rings below his eyes. Who knows what sleep is.

Latitude 5.7, longitude 102. Tonight probably 100,000 square metres burned, fire radiative power between 8.00 and 10.00. The data is not completely reliable because the clouds of smoke are so thick, the sensors can't measure accurately. Peat ground cover, a landscape that should never burn and never would on its own. To date, thousands of monkeys, a few hundred orangutans, forty Sumatran tigers and thousands upon thousands of other animals have died. The remaining now live in charred wastelands. During the last hour, an estimated further five thousand hectares have burned. The fire front's movements are shown with a delay of three to six hours; this is called near real time (NRT). The most important observation satellites orbit the world twice a day. Down here, we look up into the open sky and can't see that it's full of our machines. Images are taken regularly of every fire greater than a thousand square metres. The latest microsatellites will discover every campfire. They're the size of a refrigerator, the German operators say, and they're called Bird.

We know the pollutant clouds and their paths through the atmosphere. It could also have been a hundred thousand hectares within three hours, ten thousand orangutans—that many no longer exist—or one square kilometre with the last Sumatran tiger. He grabs his upper arms, rubbing the muscles down to his elbows hard. On nights with BMR, his entire body often twitches as if from electric shocks, but his upper arms ache most the next day, as if someone had boxed fine lacerations into the muscle fibres with small, hard fists. He has stopped tracking his sleep time. The consultant nods.

Actually, Sumatra would be coloured green on the danger map, given the rainforest. It's the only danger level that is the same in all systems, otherwise the number of levels vary, as do the colours and the terminology. On a seven-level scale, the Europeans call the highest 'very extreme danger', the Australians manage with six and call the sixth level 'catastrophic'. All use different shades of bright-to-soft shades of red, orange, yellow, dark purple and blackish-brown, green is the only colour they agree on. Green indicates hardly flammable, small risk of a fire starting or spreading. Peat gives off enormous quantities of carbon dioxide and sulphur dioxide, hundreds of thousands of people are treated for respiratory problems. The first fire was recorded more than a month ago, more are constantly being started, small fires within the inferno.

There are ten minutes left in the hour. He puts the money on the table, the consultant reaches for her appointment book. He tells her that he'll call her, that he doesn't have his datebook with him, and he doesn't care if she has noticed that he has never had a datebook because he has everything on his phone—appointments, notes, fire maps and warning services. He goes out to the street. It's hot and when he turns the nearest corner, he has to stop and support himself with one hand against the wall, bending over, his other hand on his chest. He tries not to double over as his bronchial tubes constrict ever tighter and his respiration muscles cramp. He fumbles in his trouser pockets, his jacket pockets, until he has found his inhaler, which he uses as little as possible, each time he hates it when he has no choice. Leaning on the wall, he puts the mouthpiece between his lips and inhales. He's familiar with the tears now streaming down his cheeks, they're weakness.

Day on the other side of my closed eyelids. Oblivion survives waking for a moment. Then I feel the pillowcase against my cheek, sticky and damp. Blood and wound fluid. The doctor puts the surgical instruments in a metal bowl and turns towards me on her swivel chair. For every stitch on the inner muscle layer, several on the outside to hold the skin together. It will be healed by the time you marry. The doctor says this without smiling, my lips stretch. Careful. In the bathroom mirror, my mouth is a wound. With my tongue, I feel my gums, the insides of my cheeks, when I reach the stitches, I feel stabs of pain. For at least a week you have be careful not to tear the stitches. Move your lips as little as possible. Don't speak or laugh. I turn off the bathroom light and walk through the sunlit flat. I pack a few pieces of clothing, paper, pencils and a vocabulary notebook in a travel bag. I check the stove, turn off the water, put on my sunglasses, I pick up my travel bag and sling my backpack over my shoulder.

After an hour and a half on the train, I walk onto the square in front of the small train station as the bus doors close. I push the button, which is still illuminated, and am allowed to board. I see the bus driver's face as pain shoots through mine; he turns away and drives off at the same time. I throw my arm out to hold on and drop onto a seat in the first row. A drop trickles down my chin and lands on my sternum. I reach for it and look at the blood on the tip of my forefinger. When I smile, the wound opens.

The courtyard is closed in on four sides. There's a front gate, the main entrance and a back one that leads to a meadow. My living space is on the side across from the former workshop. Although the building has only two floors and isn't very big, locals call it the castle. Years ago, an expert assessment confirmed that sections of it are in danger of collapsing; there are probably more now. No one can afford old masonry like that, they said. The room where I sleep has a blind window facing the street and one with glass panes facing the courtyard. There's a door to the adjacent room and across from it, a second, older door of unvarnished wood, to which I don't have a key and which probably leads to the entrance archway. But as long as I haven't gone through it, I won't know for sure.

Evenings I sit on the wooden bench at the back gate, next to me is a glass jar full of raisins and sunflower seeds, in the meadow a copper beech, umbrella pines, an old willow where a pond used to form after heavy rains. Farther back there's brushwood that becomes forest. To anyone who calls me, I text: Can't talk on phone right now, in writing please. To Andrea and my sister: My mouth is a wound. What happened? I fell. The doctor said it'll be healed by the time I marry. Andrea: Well then.

I eat raisins and sunflower seeds, slipping them one by one into the right corner of my mouth, sometimes the left one, too. In the meadow in front of the bench, just a step from my feet, is a burrow that is an entrance to a tunnel system at which a field mouse regularly appears. With its paws, it stuffs tiny seeds and grains into its snout, faster than I do, but I can see the similarity and I laugh. At that moment, it disappears into its burrow faster than I feel the pain and even before the pain, I feel the wetness. I reach for my mouth, blood on my fingertips, more than when I arrived with the bus, and the strain has lessened. I lean back, slip another raisin into my mouth. The mouse surfaces, disappears into the meadow and laughter peals inside me like one of those sounds in the treetops and bushes that I can't attribute to any creature or assign any meaning. I stay on the bench until it has grown dark and quiet, the blood is dry and my lips as if petrified.

In the bathroom, I bend over the sink. To remove the dried blood from my lips, I cup my hand to channel a stream of lukewarm water over my mouth. Because I can't rub them, it takes a while until the blood is washed away. A hand mirror lies next to the sink, the only mirror in the house. I don't consider the upper section of the dresser to be a mirror; it's another passageway in this room filled with doors and windows. The surface beneath it is a heavy marble slab, the dresser has stood in the same place since the castle was built. With the hand mirror, I look at the light-blue sutures in the exact centres of the upper and lower lips. On my lower lip with the deeper wound, the seam is torn open. I see the thread, the gleaming gap where the flesh has detached. I stick out my lower lip to see the inner seam. It has held. In the soft mucous membrane, there are tiny knots; I can feel the thread ends with the tip of my tongue. The stitches inside my lips, in the layers of muscles, will dissolve on their own over the next few weeks. The doctor said that my general practitioner can remove the outer stitches.

I apply tincture inside and out with a cotton swab; it burns most in the open wound. I don't move a muscle. No one has said anything about how to brush my teeth. For the time being, I dissolve a little toothpaste in the water, suck the mixture through a straw, and swish it around my mouth before letting it dribble through half-opened lips into the sink. I'm supposed to apply the tincture two to three times daily. I dab it on at least five times a day. The rust-red fluid reminds me of shed blood. After I've dabbed it on, my mouth looks like a fresh, untreated wound.

I telephone my sister and Andrea regularly. They want to hear my voice, they tell me, and I say nothing, I give a sound of assent. The way you learn not to nod wordlessly at a blind person, the two of them have quickly got used to asking me questions that can be answered with yes or no. Still, at the beginning, they always ask, how are you? The habit is ingrained, but they move on to other questions right away. Has the swelling gone down? Has the pain lessened? What are you eating? With a straw, moving my lips as little as possible. What? My sister considers a while, oh right. Usually there's no need to repeat anything, it's enough for them to think about what they heard. She goes through what can be eaten through a straw. You could make yourself some broth. I make my noise of assent, a throaty sound in a middle range, soothing, low, higher, low. Sometimes I repeat it, and it works as an encouragement to keep talking or as a signal of interest or sympathy, depending on how I colour and on what the other person is talking about. Apple sauce. Porridge, no, that's too thick. Do you have an immersion blender? My sister laughs. If she were here, she could prepare the same food for me and her child, who's slowly recovering, she tells me.

There's a shop in the next village, a forty minutes' walk away, longer on the walk home with my purchases on my back. I still have a package of raisins, two bottles of wine, sunflower seeds, six containers of yoghurt. I drink the wine from a small water glass today with a light-pink straw. The cigarette is a little thicker, but I can manage. I tried a cigarette holder, the flattened mouthpiece fits neatly between my lightly parted lips, but it means taking a harder drag than on a cigarette alone. I have to avoid tensing my muscles. I only take a light drag, I keep the smoke in my mouth before I let it escape between the upper and lower stitches. The smoke drifts away. I hold my hand with the cigarette at shoulder height, my elbow propped on my hip. Nothing moves.

The day birds have fallen silent. Unnoticed by me, the blackbird has broken off its endless variations, the raucous sparrows have flown away. They must have stopped one by one, some earlier than others. One has to be the last, but I've never been able to catch it, the day's last birdcall, the onset of silence. The crows are the last, he told me. You can hear their noise when they gather high in a tree for the night and when they've fallen silent on some secret signal, you can see their noiseless shapes, black against the night sky, as long as there's a little light left. I only see crows alone, during the day. I don't know where their sleeping tree is.

I never linger in the space between my bedroom and kitchen, it's just a passage for me. All the windows look out over the courtyard, I think, whenever I think of the castle, but it's not true. In the kitchen, a small square opening has been left the outside wall, and it reveals the how thick the wall is. A tiny window with a warped wooden frame that hasn't closed for years. The elder and blackberry bushes growing outside it stick their twigs and tendrils inside. On the large wooden table in the kitchen are paper, pens and a vocabulary notebook. To read anything on the paper, you have to turn on the light at any hour of the day. I prefer to open the door that leads to the courtyard to disperse the semi-darkness over the table.

At night I lie in bed—a cast-iron frame with tall posts—between the doors to the left and right, the window onto the courtyard over my head and across from the blind one onto the street. I cover the mirror on the dresser every night with a cloth that is often gone in the morning. A breeze is enough to lift the thin silk fabric and let it fall onto the marble below. The doors and window must leak; the air in the room is in constant motion. There's a draught, as they say. I wait until my heart rate slows, the throbbing in my lips is weaker. I listen. Outside the night is warm, inside it's always cool. The hair on my arms rises first. The shoulder blades, small bone plates, emerge under the fur, with every step one rises, the other sinks deeper.

What do you see? the mother asked when she came to the side of the bed in which the child lay with eyes wide open. The walls absorb everything, have for several centuries now. The hour of the wolf is in deepest night and doesn't have anything to do with darkness. Shadows can be light, luminous even. No need to be afraid. The child isn't afraid. She was left exposed and stood firm. Observed all the vows of silence that had been imposed on her. Don't look so angry. Then you learn you have to speak and to smile.

You're going to have to look gloomy for a while, the doctor had said, but then your smile will be all the prettier afterwards. Late afternoon, I go shopping. Knapsack on my back, wearing a straw hat on my head and a kerchief around my neck. The fields on either side of the road are replaced by construction sites, then single-family homes. Cars park on the square in front of the church, notices are hung in a glass-fronted case, those of the parish in the right side, those of the community in the left. Free self-defence classes for women and girls. Sunday mass will now be held at 16.00.

In the store it's cool, my face burns. The owner is stocking the shelves from a shopping cart filled with long-life milk, cans of cat food and bags of granulated sugar. He has grown old, his movements slow, his hair grey. Hello. He answers before looking up, a fleeting glance that gets caught, turns away, returns, stays turned away. The pang in my underlip was almost soft, the tension has released. I greet the owner's wife sitting behind the counter with bread, sausage, cheese. She looks at my face, she says nothing. Do you have a tissue? I ask. She gives me a white napkin, with which I dab the blood from my lips, a piece of scab and rust-red tincture. I ask for a roll and also purchase some raisins, yoghurt, apple sauce, white wine, cigarettes. The man keeps his gaze lowered as he types in the prices. Sunflower seeds. He doesn't react, again, sunflower seeds, I make an effort to speak clearly with a questioning tone. Maybe in the storehouse, he says without looking up and points to the red number on the cash register. As I pack up my knapsack, he turns away to put the newspapers in order. Goodbye.

Back in the castle, I put the yoghurt and white wine in the refrigerator and go out the back gate. I want to share the fresh bread with the mouse. I tear the roll down the middle, from the soft insides I make little pellets, which I alternately toss in front of the burrow entrance and slip into the corner of my mouth. The mouse will come when I'm gone. I'll be back before it gets dark, I say softly. I wash down the rest of the roll with water and tie my shoes.

I catch a movement in one of the dusty windowpanes of the castle's workshop wing as I pass. I turn the wooden latch on the entrance gate and go back to get the key from the kitchen sideboard. I leave the key in the lock and pull the door closed from the outside. I take a supply road that runs between the fields and reach the main road. The straw hat sways back and forth on its string against my back. Sweat drips from my philtrum over my upper lip and into the wound, the sun burns the salt into it. I remain standing where the field road forks. The frog pond is some way up the hill. It's too small and thick with algae and lily pads to swim in, but you can slip into it and spread your arms out just below the surface between the aquatic plants. After your dip, you can dry off in the sun and let the gnats and horseflies collect their toll of blood.

In this section, the dirt-field road has been paved; I hear voices from a distance. Not far from the pond an area has been levelled and a table and bench installed. Four, five, six guys, two of them perched on the backrest, with motorcycles around them. The voices don't resolve into a conversation, but clash, one regularly rises above the others only to stop abruptly, interrupted. I'm close enough to see the cigarette butts on the ground and for them to notice me. They continue talking, cautiously now, their gazes uneasy, then only one is speaking, almost to himself. Hi all, I say with a hint of a smile, the cut on my lower lip opens slightly, enough for a few drops of blood but without tearing open any wider. After I've passed them, the one who'd kept talking says hello, and the silence surrounding his stammering continues as I leave the pond behind. Here the path is unpaved again; it rises steeply along a line of pine trees. The voices at my back drill upwards, I walk with firm strides until I can no longer hear them.

I step between the trees, a narrow strip that functions as a border and a windbreak, a hunting blind, above me a woodpecker. I tilt my head back to listen until it stops, behind us is a rumbling. I walk along the edge of the field, high up in his driver's cab, a man with a red, sweat-covered face, hand raised in greeting. I reach the forest's edge on the hill crest and look back. The heavy agricultural machines move slowly over the fields, a short distance away, cars pass rapidly and silently on the main road. Glancing around once more like a thief who then disappears without a sound through the already opened door into a house that isn't his. In the forest, I take careful steps as if I could remain unnoticed. Trunk, bark, leaves, mosses, mushrooms. In my trouser pocket, a palm-sized notebook, a pencil as long as a pinky. Soon enough, I come upon a forest path, a sign, dumping debris is forbidden.

In the darkness, I squat on the edge of the field, lights shimmering ahead of me, a brightly lit field. Below me, the warmth of my steaming urine, a stamping comes through the ground, not a sound, just a rhythmic vibration against the soles of my feet. I move my arm to figure out where it is. Each movement brings a vague nausea, as if my arm was connected to my stomach. The sound of my palm rubbing the sheet. The sound of heavy tractor wheels and the rattle of a plough penetrate the surface of the asphalt, through the deeper layers, and through the blind window. Being awake increases the nausea.

A faint something follows me throughout the morning, brushes my shoulder again and again, and every time I turn my head seeing nothing, until suddenly, as I'm taking a yoghurt out of the fridge, my face appears in the hand mirror. The fingers of my right hand, stroking my right cheek, and my voice murmurs, something . . . My fingers wash off the dirt, apply tincture with a cotton ball, first on my upper lip, then on my lower lip. A dark trace in the sink, I don't know if I was earth or rust, now I hear footsteps, but I don't turn around.

On a wooden fence near the path is a young falcon that doesn't fly away and I finally can classify the scream I've been hearing for a while, shrill, at regular intervals, not too often so as not to attract other hunters but still to call its mother. It makes no sound while I look at it, doesn't move. Not a step closer. The perfectly marked face and curved beak. It waits until I've gone a considerable distance off before it makes another cry. I want to take the wide forest road to a trail I noticed a few days ago, a game trail leading into the thick underbrush. I stop on the road and look up. A thick bundle of sunbeams falls through the treetops, a column of light, in which hoverflies have gathered. Occasionally one rises, pauses, sinks again, then they all hover again in the same spot. At the fork, there's a signpost with place names, maps of hiking trails and a shield with a black symbol and the words: Video-Monitored.

The tourist office is located behind the church in the town hall. The eyes of the woman behind the counter flit back and forth between my mouth and my eyes, from my eyes to the door behind me and back again, trying to keep her eyes on mine. I ask about the video monitoring, she smiles. For two years we've been working on security for the hiking trail network, a huge project. She picks out some brochures and unfolds a map on the counter. Unfortunately, it's still not complete, but here—she points with her finger—you see the trails for which cameras have already been installed. I want to know if the cameras are mounted on trees, with nails or cables, and how often they're serviced. She's not sure. The woman looks at the counter without a word. But here, she says laying a finger on the map and looking at my mouth, is the emergency number for the police. There's no reason to be afraid in our forest. I catch her eye and hold it. You think so? I smile. Scabs feel different than skin. The thin new skin on my upper lip tears, the scab on my lower lip breaks. Fresh blood and wound fluid. No pus, I keep the wound clean. I fold up the map with the light-red drop inside and thank her. Do you need a tissue? she calls when I'm already at the door. I wave the map without turning around.

On the street through the village, there's a large traffic island with a landmarked chapel. In front of it are two benches, a panel with the history of the building, three young trees that throw no shade and can't grow here. I let the sun dry my wound as I study the map. I start with the yellow trail, which includes the path where I saw the shield. I don't meet anyone, either on foot or on a bicycle, or any forestry workers. At a few forks in the road I see the shield with the symbol and the words Video-Monitored, I often see larger signs that designate the trails, now and again an old tree encircled with a wire and on it a sign saying Natural Treasure. On many more trees, far above my head, metal plaques with nothing decipherable on them have been mounted with nails. What I call forest is an area management zone with the proceeds from every square centimetre calculated. Deer run off a distance only to start browsing again. Glaring spray-painted markings   designate trees that will be felled.

I get fewer calls and messages. The silence increases, as does the heat. If I sit long enough on the bench outside the back gate, I sometimes forget, but then I want to moisten my dry lips with my tongue and I feel the sutures. I have larger plastic straws for thicker liquids, thin ones for drinks. Mostly, I stick them in the right corner of my mouth—even drinking with straws is governed by righthandedness. When I drink from the left side of my mouth, I often drink too quickly and choke. I let the coffee get lukewarm; it can't be hot. I've learnt that my lips test the temperature of any food or drinks before they reach the inside of my mouth. It's as if my sense of taste were wounded along with my lips or as if all my senses were concentrated on the wound: pain, taste and smell. Sometimes I hold my breath because I smell decay. Everything I consume through the plastic straw tastes bland and stale, the coffee is watery, I can't taste the difference between vanilla and strawberry yoghurt. The reason I rarely feel hungry is probably due to the raisins, which I eat in huge quantities. Most intense are the sweetness of dried berries and the tartness of white wine. It has to be chilled. I hold the liquid in my mouth until it has warmed; the tartness is a faint burning on my wound.

When he leaves work late in the evening, the night watchman is sometimes smoking outside the building and offers him a cigarette and lights it. He holds the cigarette between his fingers until it has burned down. He prefers talking about the weather with the night watchman than talking with his colleagues. Something's not right here, the night watchman says, what do you think? He has a small garden on the outskirts of the city and the severe weather recently destroyed all his vegetable plants, nonetheless the ground is dry. He dug down at least a metre, and the dirt there wasn't even moist. That's very odd, the night watchman says and tells him goodnight. He walks away from the institute along the hills in a southernly direction. Before the road's steep descent, he stops and looks out over the city. There's not a cloud in the sky, the distant range of hills to the east is distinctly visible, the night will be clear. It was the last workday before his holiday, he has worked enough overtime to take a week off. Before leaving, he'd updated the hazard map. He turns around, gazes up at the forested hillsides. He has been observing an area in the east of the country for some time now. What do you do when you have a week off? the consultant asks.

Over several days with no wind, the ground fire has spread unnoticed in the top layer of humus. Within hours it has grown into a raging fire no one could have anticipated. It can't ever be anticipated, or rather, it always can since in the great majority of cases the cause is human error. What they could have known was that the forest was highly flammable there. Drought, an accumulation of fuel, pine and spruce stands. A crown fire can leap over all obstacles, fire lanes, roads and rivers when the wind rises. On top of this, a fire makes its own storm. The flames sail through the air, fire clouds produce lightning but any precipitation is vapourized before it even comes close to the ground.

A black clearing opens before me; nothing remains of the grass, bushes and tree seedlings. The area had just been reforested after having burned several times in recent years. The ground is filled with munitions, each year brings new explosions. They use the term 'total loss' when the trees are completely destroyed and 'lethal damages' when they die in the fire. I reach a section of old stand, the young trees are completely burnt, a few charred stumps of the old ones remain. The buffer zones created with the regular ploughing under of vegetation and humus that stop the fire are still recognizable. The earth stirred up by heavy emergency vehicles, steps of firefighters in full gear, equipment. Forestry management calls the area along the tree line where certain trees survive the combat zone.

I've lost my sense of direction. I don't know if I'm still on a hill or have already reached the lower plain. I finally come out of the forest unexpectedly onto a field, a road. A few buildings and a car turning into a driveway. The driver gets out, I greet him from some distance, stop at the electric gate on the border of his property. The man turns, key ring in hand, watches as I approach. From head to toe and back to my face. Before leaving, I applied fresh tincture. Could he tell me how to get to the castle, I ask him. I don't say castle, though, I say the name of the village. He looks me over once again and at my feet. Along the road or off? I ask for both options. Not a sound behind me after I turn to leave, then the rattle of keys. My left breast is heavier than my right, sweat gathers beneath it, I feel the fold of my skin at every step. I go back on a broad forest road, slow, tired. At dusk, I reach the meadow by the back gate. In the dark kitchen, I stand mutely at the table. On it, my vocabulary notebook and next to it, the smaller one, warm and damp from my trouser pocket.

No fire training today, he says, I mean the one with light. Breathing is difficult for him, every inhalation is a conscious act, with every exhalation he makes an effort to breathe out as much used air as possible. The consultant stands up, goes to the window and opens it as wide as the plants allow. Would you like to do some other exercise? He sets his fingertips on the cool glass tabletop, then on his swollen eyelids covering his aching eyes. Mostly he wants to stop feeling her gaze on his ravaged face. There's no medical explanation for how sleep deprivation makes your eyes burn; she confirmed this and smiled when he said that with all the smoke and gasses, Hell is no place for asthmatics. The consultant takes the mats from the corner behind her desk. The first time, he offered to help but she declined; since then, he waits for her to invite him with a hand gesture.

As long as he keeps seeing the consultant, he's seeking relief. The promised salvation is one day to be able to sleep as before. The consultant observes him discreetly, as if by chance. He knows she is evaluating him, creating an idea for herself of his appearance, posture, body language. No one can read the signs of sleep disorders better than she can. The restlessness and the control it takes to resist giving into the false signs that can come from overstimulation. Not starting or flinching when you see from the corner of your eye something approaching that turns out not to be there. The restraint of the utterly exhausted, who no longer trust their own senses. Remaining excessively still because they constantly want to escape. His lips are also cracked, torn at the corners of his mouth from the inhaler that he now has to use more often when he climbs the hill to the Meteorological Institute.

He's meant to help improve the alert system. The goal is thorough monitoring of the forest. They want to know what's growing in it and understand the composition and moisture levels of all the soil layers, the aridity of the vegetation—forest floor, understory, canopy and emergent layer—and everything about its breathing. What the air is composed of and in what proportions the forest exhales and inhales the air, what it retains and what it transforms from the air. Everywhere in the world, ever-more complex measuring stations and higher towers are being built to assess the forest as a sink and source of pollutants. It's not about the health of the forest but of humans. The forest is examined from the lower, middle and upper atmospheres, equipment is brought in and calculations are made far away. No one has any idea of the extent to which it's monitored. No single person can oversee all the measurements which can't be represented in their totality either mentally or physically.

Feel your body on the mat. Feel where it's supported, how heavy it is. Let your body sink into the mat. The back of his head is like lead that retains warmth for a long time. Feel the breath stream through your nose, your throat, your ribcage. He listens to the droning in his chest while the consultant talks about the abdomen, the pelvis, the legs. He looks at the bookshelf from which a book protrudes precariously, a diagnostic manual, at least two thousand pages of fine print. The consultant has reached the head again. Feel your breath in the space under your eyes, your sinuses, let your breath stream in and out, bring your attention to your forehead. Imagine sensation growing lighter under your skull, she says. He wishes the diagnostic manual would kill him. It should hit him in the pit of his stomach, to finally knock the wind out of him.

The glowing rectangle on his knees shows the orbits of the earth's observation satellites. The earth is swathed in bands, strip upon strip, next to each other, overlapping each other. Is the monitoring truly complete? There are always gaps. At least, he still wants to think so. He sits and studies the map for a while, before going to the window and leaning out, his gaze fixed on the sky, eyes tainted by the light from his screen. He goes outside and looks for the widest and darkest street where he can stand and tilt his head back. He knows there's no cloud cover tonight, yet few stars are visible and even though he waits for a while they don't increase. Immeasurability slips farther away, the more stubbornly we pursue it.

He had every printer in the institute run throughout the night. When his colleagues arrived in the morning, the corridor to his room as well as the floor of his office were covered with a thick layer of paper. And this is only the data from three earth observation satellites this week. He refuses to participate in the project to improve the forest monitoring. What he wants is utopian, he's told. A new kind of forest management, educating the population, foresters, forest rangers and forest dwellers. You really spoke about forest dwellers? Going forward, the Meteorological Institute will work together with insurers. Risks must be reassessed, all damages can't be covered as they have been until now. The night watchman, whom he occasionally kept company with a cigarette, died out of the blue. In fact, he checked—the watchman died on a day with zero per cent cloud coverage.

He asks if he can take over the position of night watchman; he'd prefer it to sick leave. How would that look, him sitting in the watchman's lodge, his boss wants to know, but his boss gives in when he says he'll resign otherwise. No one is as well trained in the field—until recently forest fires were seen as exotic in these parts. At the institute, they're hoping he'll come to his senses soon, he's told. Behind his back, they talk of burnout.

Went to bed at midnight, 1 PLS at 1.00, 1 ½ PLS at 2.30, got up around 3.30, lay down again at 5.00, dozed, up at 6.00; went to bed at 23.00, light out around 0.30, didn't sleep, up at 3.00, lay down around 5.00, up at 6.00; went to bed at midnight, 2 ½ PLS, probably fell asleep around 1.00, woke at 3.30, lay awake, up around 5.30; Lat. 48.1929 Lon. 16.361, home at 5.30, lay down, up at 6.30; went to bed at 23.30, 2 PLS, light sleep until around 2.00, up, lay down again at 3.30, no sleep, up at 5.00, to bed 00.00, prob. dozed, up at 4.00, lay back down at 5.00, slept, up with alarm 6.00; BT 1.00, no sleep, up 4.30, Lat. 43.826 Long. 6.507, FWI < 25, DMC+DC!, didn't lie down again; bed 00.00, 3 PLS, prob. aslp around 5.00, up 6.00; bed 23.00, light out 00.00, no sleep until around 3.00, prob. dozed, up 4.15, lay down 5.30, up 6.00; bed 00.00, 1 PLS, lay awake, 2 PLS 2.30, prob. dozed, up 4.00, lay down 5.30, alarm, up 6.30; bed 23.30, no PLS, Lat. 43.826 Long. 6.507, FWI 45, lay awake, prob. aslp around 5.00, alarm, up 6.00; bed 23.00, 2 PLS, fell aslp quickly, up 1.30, no S until 2.30, got up, glob. burn. intensity high, lay down 4.30, prob. aslp around 5.30, alarm, up 6.00, bed 00.00, 2 P, up 5.00, got up 5.30; bed 00.00, no S, up 3.00, lay down 5.00, got up 6.00; bed 23.00, no S; bed 23.30, 3 P, aslp, awake 4.30, bed 1.00, slept a little at some point, prob. 4 hrs, got up 8.00; bed 23.30, prob aslp 23.30, up 4.00, lay down 5.30, prob. 1 hr S; 2 P at 23.30, up 4.00, Daily Total FRP EU+UK > 29; 2 PLS 00.00, dozed until 1.00, 1

PLS 1.30, no S; NSW ATC West. Austr. catastrophic, up 3.00, lay down 5.00, no S, got up 6.30; BT 3.00, prob. S, up 5.00, 43,000 ha.; BT 00.00, 1 ½ PLS 1.00, 1 ½ PLS 2.00, prob. dozed betw 3.00 and 4.30; 00.00 3 PLS, S halluc., Lat 48.294 Long 16.681, wind gusts 97, up 5.45, lay down 00.00 2 P, slept till around 4.00, up 6.00, 2 PLS 23.00, 2 PLS 0.30, up 3.00, lay down 5.30, up 6.00, home 2.00, Lat 48 Long 16 FRP 9.28 confidence n, prob slept 2.30–6.00, -9.7677 120.5579 FRP 436, -9.7693 120.5697 FRP 117.7, -9.7671 120.5635 FRP 290.8, GMR, no S, prob. dozed 0.30 to 2.00, dspr, 2 P, up, lay down 4.30, up 5.30, Fire Dist. Record borealis, GMR, no S, 4 PLS, 00.00, 2 P, GMR, 2.00 3 PLS, dspr, no D, no S, up 4.00, dspr, down 00.00, prob dzd 1.00–3.00, up, Lat-Lng -8.35-116.7 Lat-Lng -10.11-123.35, down 5.00, up 6.00, dspr, 2 P, n S, n S, n S, 3 P 00.00 dzd until 5.30, up 6.00, n S, n S, dspr.

His forehead the night sky, expanding with each breath. With each inhalation the sky grows wider, with each exhalation it grows smaller. An earthworm, deep in the ground, ever-less oxygen, ever-greater warmth, the whistling softer and softer. He lies in extreme respiratory distress somewhere in a hospital and I'm searching a large-format book with thousands of densely printed pages for where it is I'll find him. I'll recognize the name when I see it, I quickly leaf through the pages, searching my memory at the same time. A double letter, a soft consonant, east and west, that much I know, an area enveloped in thick, black smoke. If only he didn't always go after peat fires. The saddest fires are the ones that are lit through violence. They burn against their will, where they shouldn't even be, the way children pass on the atrocities inflicted on them. Someone has to feel for them as well. Someone has to bear the sadness. The saddest fires are the primeval forest fires.

He has stretched out on the bed, I lay down next to him and in the silence, I hear the faint whistling with every exhalation. You should use your inhaler. And you should stop smoking. He turns his face towards me. Our breaths are too short, together we could lengthen them a little. We hold each other's shoulders to sink deeper. Gills can absorb more oxygen underwater than human lungs from the atmosphere. Counter-current exchange means that two opposed circulatory systems are semipermeable and can feed each other. Inhalation a high-pitched whistling, exhalation a humming. A polyphonic wheezing. Inhaling from the mouth through the back of the head and through the ribcage into the back. Shoulder blades and all lobes of the lungs rise and fall with every breath. With each inhalation, the abdominal wall expands, submits to the sacrum that flexes towards it; they move apart with each exhalation. Hands in front of the torso to scoop air into the mouth, into the throat, the bronchial tubes, the ribcage expands.

West Nusa Tenggara and East Nusa Tenggara. The fire's centre has shifted to the province east of Sumatra. Because it hadn't burned there in the past, they have almost no firefighting personnel or equipment. The dryness readings of the upper-soil layers have reached improbable levels for a rainforest. The number of dark-red squares increases daily, others turn light red and orange, then yellow. On European maps, they'll turn blue when the fire has burned longer than seven days. But this is no indication of their intensity.

Mornings, I sit on a chair against the wall next to the entrance of my living space, near where I sleep. I watch the blackbird that has built a nest in the Virginia creeper above my head and is searching for food in the meadow. I stick the green plastic straw in the right corner of my mouth and suck the almost cold coffee from the cup. Once I've sat long enough for the morning sun to light up my dreams, I go inside and, dazzled by the sunlight, sit at the kitchen table and write blindly. Someone knocked on the window and I woke up and saw a forearm above me. I stretched the hand that is writing now out to the left, raised my right shoulder from the mattress and turned it, along with my head and neck, towards the wall.

A blow outside on the blind window, the light bricks in the thick stone. It wasn't a knock, the way you rap with your knuckles before entering a room or a house, a more-or-less rhythmic sequence in the certainty that you'll be welcome; this was no obliging knocking. Shooting up from the bushes against the outside wall, a single blow with the heel of a hand and sliding fingertips, hastily, in distress, then hurriedly blending one's own shadow into the larger darkness. I sank back into sleep because I didn't know what woke me, now I remember.

I leave the kitchen table and go into the courtyard, to the front gate. I lift the wooden latch from the holder, then stand in the driveway and look up and down the street. Across the meadow to the wall of the building. I stroke the outside surface of the blind window, lay my hand flat on it, the wall here is smoother and more even compared to the old wall around it. I walk along the wall down to the corner. The blackberry bush has grown up to the bottom edge of the roof, soon it will start to overgrow the house. I push the thorny vines aside to see the kitchen window. Blackberry and elderberry bushes have grown together with other bushes into impenetrable shrubbery, which must be hiding the meadow I look at in evenings. In one spot that consists primarily of tangles without thorns, I discover an opening that someone has already slipped through, above the ground, about knee-height. As I push my way through the roots and twigs, I realize that there's no sound of motors. Or of birds, which must live here in this thicket.

An area I've never seen before. A copse, I think, but I don't see any trees. I wade through grass that reaches my hips in some spots; in between are tufts of fern that shouldn't grow in the blazing heat of the sun and remain still—even when I touch them, they don't tremble. The ground under the hollow growth is uneven, with my feet I feel small ridges, invisible lines. The black remains of tree trunks on which no mushrooms grow. A flat, silky surface, the coal dust blends with the thin film of sweat on my skin.

He has been watching fire since he came into this world. In natural flames, the proportion of blue light is small, mostly overshadowed by the red and yellow sections. When wood burns with a large enough supply of air, the flames are fat, golden-yellow, bright to half-transparent depending on the time of day, depending on the sunlight. Shielding my eyes with my hand, I peer through the dusty pane of glass. I don't have a key to the workshop wing. If there is one, it's not with the others on the kitchen sideboard. Inside it's dim. I can make out crates and barrels, wooden shelves on the walls, a table, equipment pushed together. In the corner a brick oven, deeper in the room a shape, feed or grain, seeds or a duffel bag, a travel case. A huddled figure. 'Settling in' is the expression people around here use. They're constantly worried that someone could surreptitiously become a local.

Black fingerprints remain on the wall where I'd braced myself and I take a few steps towards the middle of the courtyard. At this hour of the day, when the sun rises above the east wall, its light falls through the open door directly into the kitchen. I look at my unmade bed through the bedroom window that opens inwardly. On the marble dresser top, the towel. The mirror is a bright surface. In the bathroom, I apply tincture on my upper lip, on my lower lip, inside and out, and on the long scratch on my right forearm.

Aren't you lonely? Andrea asks. I see the mouse disappear down its hole and make a negating sound, two short intonations. How lucky you are to be in the countryside. I make my affirming sound. What do you do all day? Nothing. Moving my lips as little as possible, tonelessly. I hear the concern. There's a way to laugh that almost completely avoids any tensing of the facial muscles, it comes from the ribcage, rolls up through the throat and tickles the roof of the mouth, a round, clear sound. I laugh. All right, then. Now Andrea laughs too. I hold the telephone a little farther away from my ear. I'm becoming more and more sensitive. She can arrange to visit me. I make my sound. Your holiday? Reducing every response to the absolute minimum. I can't remember most of what I said in earlier conversations. Not easy, Andrea says, but there's been some progress. We've talked a lot. Basque country, he was in his element.

The mouse emerges from the burrow near my feet and sets off over the meadow. There was one very good afternoon, Andrea says. I was all by myself. First in the museum, then a drink on the square, it was lovely. I talked with someone who was sitting alone and with the waiter who joined in. They said my Spanish was flawless. I wouldn't have wanted him there at all. I probably didn't think of him once for two hours, Andrea says. She often remembers this moment. How strong she felt. Her therapist had advised to do it very consciously. The mouse returns, senses danger, freezes and disappears into its hole. I know it sounds like NLP, but that's the way our brain works. Now I see clearly that I have a problem with intimacy, Andrea says. But as long as he's distant, I can say it's because of him. Laughter. I listen to Andrea talk. I watch the mouse that has re-emerged from its hole. It probably has its young hidden in an underground nest, a few steps from my feet. Andrea falls silent. Sad? I hear her make a movement, light a cigarette, exhale smoke. Very tired, she says, sometimes. And then she has to go. I'm thinking of you, sending you a hug. I make my affirming noise, softly, several times in a row so that it becomes a sound.

I tap the red telephone icon, then again for longer, to turn the phone off. I place the phone next to me on the bench, next to the jar with raisins and sunflower seeds, the last remaining ones. I sprinkle a few in front of the burrow entrance. Daylight still shines from behind the hill after sunset, trickling out of the air that had been saturated with it for hours. A shadow at the burrow hole. Good night. I cool off the inside of my mouth and my wound with white wine. Light my last cigarette of the day. I hold the smoke in my lungs and let it slowly seep out through the small gap between my sutures until dizziness sets in.

In the dark, I walk out into the meadow where I can't see the earth under my feet, its pull feels weaker and my limbs lighter. My outstretched hands are delineated in sharp contrast. The Meteorological Institute is careful to avoid light pollution, the footpath from the main building to the back of the premises is lit only with dim, knee-high lamps. Across the dark, open space to the measurement tower. Hand on the railing, a thin iron bar, five flights of ten tall stairs. Footsteps cause the structure to sway slightly, every gust of wind is transmitted to the body as motion. He climbs without looking down, having reached the platform, he stands in the centre among the instruments. The only firm contact in this air space is with the metal grate under his feet. His brain seeks evidence, aims through his eyes at the distant lights, at the lines that depending on the weather and the phase of the moon, indicate the horizon. On dark nights, it's possible for your sense of direction to falter and bring on the urge to lower your head to the floor. Tonight is not a dark night, twenty-five per cent cloud cover and the moon is two-thirds full. The ridge of hills to the east is clearly visible.

My invisible feet take inaudible steps. I don't sit at the kitchen table to write entries, I stand in the dark. You're going to ruin your eyesight, children are told. It's bright in the bathroom, the white of the walls and the tiles intensify the light from the bulb. In the hand mirror, I look at my lips and the scab-covered stitches. Using two fingers, I carefully move my lower lip back and forth until a little fluid is released and moistens the wound. I turn off the light. With my hands, I find the cool marble top, the silk cloth, feel for the mirror and prop it between the wooden frame and the wall before I get into bed. My eyes, which always try to make out something familiar in the darkness, find the straw hat with the wide brim, a light, round spot next to one of the doors. Avoid direct sunlight, the doctor had advised me, because of scarring.

I usually leave the castle through the front gate. I don't fasten the latch any more, there's no wind to move the doors. I don't meet anyone and there's not a single open door nor open window on the houses. Instead of curtains, many people now have shutters, which don't move. A few cars drive past and no one works in the fields on a holiday. The landscape without the drone of machines. I take unmarked trails and wander along the edge of the forest. I notice an uncultivated strip between corn and stubble fields and presume there's a body of water under the green. I can hear it when I'm near, a stream overgrown with bushes, grass and trees. I cross it at a section with sparse vegetation, in front of me ducklings start up, flee noisily to the lower branch of a tree. The thin stream in the furrow below me, behind me the grass and reeds spring back up, rustling.

A rabbit darts away over the stubble field. I sit on the overgrown path on the field's edge, false mayweed and corn poppies grow intertwined. Ants leave burning red spots on my legs. I take my palm-sized notebook that is pressing against my hip from my pocket. I haven't seen a single camera so far. For a sense of security, signs are enough, they say. Or it's about something else. Don't forget that the forest is property, and a fire means property damage. There are new instruments whose measurements the Meteorological Institute wants to analyse without knowing how to use them. They're called tools, plastic panels no bigger than a book, well camouflaged, different models for different kinds of forests. One for every square metre measures the humidity, temperature, air composition and pollution levels. In addition, not visible from outside, small cameras that automatically change viewing angles at regular intervals.

I approach the castle from the back. I catch sight of it from one of the surrounding slopes, from the top of a hill, and plan a route along roads, paths, unploughed strips, fields, to the last stretch of forest that will lead me straight to the meadow next to the back gate. I stay at higher elevations as long as possible, repeatedly searching for a lookout point, confirming my route, until I'm so close I can no longer see the castle. I have stored in my memory the contours of the hills, the shape of their crests, the configuration of the various kinds of vegetation and isolated groups of trees and have gained an understanding of the brightness between their trunks, how the light shines through them, in order to gauge the density of the forest and the terrain behind it.

But in the last stretch of the forest, I'm constantly mistaken. Where I assume I'll find an exit in less densely wooded places, I end up in a dim conifer plantation, and where I least expect it, the thicket opens up. One time, I unexpectedly landed in a swampy section with dwarf birch and horsetail that I wouldn't find a second time. I don't recognize anything here, except when I look around and suddenly see the beech grove, a surprise every time. The ground still retains traces of the oak trees that grew here for many centuries. From the forest, I step out onto the meadow, first glimpsing the tall crowns of the umbrella pines, then the weeping willow, the copper beech, the back gate, the blackberry bush. A withered apple tree growing naturally outside the orchard, the passageway.

What was once a retaining wall has fallen apart and the small hut with only one window and one door has also been brought down by weather and blackberry bushes. Inside it, a rough wooden table, two benches, a plank bed, the cauldron and the oven underneath, glass tubes out of which the clear liquid flowed. They ran the still in the evening and into the night. That night was the fire's element is something he knew as young child, the fact that he was taught the four elements—which didn't include day or night—made no difference. He later learnt that the old teachings about the elements had been superseded and fire downgraded to a reaction. He learnt the periodic table and that vegetation fires burn most intensely during the day, yet he secretly maintained his belief that fire belonged to the night.

Smoke warms, they said, and in late frosts they placed under the trees wheelbarrows filled with wood chips, as damp as possible so they would burn slowly and give off a lot of smoke. The child sat on the doorstep of the orchard hut and kept vigil. He was still small and too delicate, they said, and none of them suspected that he wasn't in bed but instead, when the cold became too much, he would sit near a wheelbarrow under a tree so that he, too, could get warm. The smoke enveloped him thickly and yet wasn't enough to keep the warmth in the ground and in the trees on that ice-cold night. The frost was stronger than expected and the cherry crop was meagre that year.

It's a question of self-worth, Andrea says. I hold the telephone to my left ear. Tiny breadcrumbs at the entrance to the burrow. You know what I mean? She doesn't expect an answer, I fell on my mouth, I don't have to talk any more. My sounds—questioning, affirmative, expectant, reassuring—are enough, and Andrea never asks if she's understood one correctly or what I meant with another. I have to believe that my little life has some meaning, otherwise I won't do anything any more. Andrés is gone. Even though he never lived in the same city or even the same country, he's gone. The mouse appears, sniffs in all directions and starts to fortify the entrance, the burrow's walls and the ramp that serves as her lookout. Otherwise, I'll lose the courage to face life. I hear Andrea light another cigarette and I take a drag on mine. The smoke burns a little, blood throbs under the thin new skin of my upper lip. I repeat the word courage, articulate it slowly, the way you pronounce a word in a foreign language for the first time.

Others treat you the way you treat yourself, don't you think? Andrea lights another cigarette. I picture her when fear gets the better of her. Sitting in an armchair, framed by the backrest, the arms and the seat, she can stay calm for a while. As soon as she gets up, she starts tidying. When she can't find anything to do, she brushes the cloth on her upper arms, down the sides of her hips, the way you smoothen a skirt. The closer she is to a room's centre, the farther away all objects are from her, and in the worst cases, she begins to wring her hands. Yes, I say. I hear her exhale smoke again, stub out her cigarette in the ashtray. Thanks, she says, it was helpful talking to you. I hang up, place the phone on the bench next to me and picture Andrea sitting still as the light fades, the mouse runs away and returns and we both remain silent.

Memory of a sound, this time on glass. The bitter taste on my gums. Not having to speak. Soft tugging on the threads. A reflection flashes on the dresser when I look at it, the silk cloth on the marble top, fallen. I open both panels of the window facing the courtyard and turn my head towards the entrance gate, and I see something white. Brightness fills the courtyard. The remains of the night dissipates as the sun rises. In the bathroom I apply the tincture liberally, spreading the rust-red liquid inside and out, over the wound.

He doesn't flinch at the sight of a flame, unlike most people, re-enacting the movement that once followed the very first pain. In his case, the movement follows the pain and he takes his hand away. When handling animals, you also learn to avoid violent gestures and how to interpret their sounds: a hiss is different than a purr. He has to take care not to put his hand into the mouth of the oven to push the glowing pieces of wood farther back. When he doesn't pay attention, he nudges the burning hot lid with his right hand over the opening, holding the poker in his left hand like a useless, unfamiliar object. At a campfire, he rummages with bare hands in the coals to pick out the potatoes. He doesn't throw branches and bits of wood into the fire from a safe distance, just as you wouldn't throw dinner onto a table. Occasionally, his sleeve begins to smoulder and burn, all of his shirt cuffs have black borders or holes. But it has been a long time since he's sat by a campfire, he hates it when fires are lit as pastimes. Campfires are justified as a means of survival, so you can warm, feed or protect yourself from wild animals when necessary.

There are old, unwritten rules, which he follows. He knows how fires start and how they spread, he just sometimes forgets his own, vulnerable body. Superficial burn wounds are areas of strangely smooth skin, deeper burns are engraved, scars without lacerations or stitches. His hands show no signs of surgeries, they change with each new burn, the ways stones and the ground are constantly being shaped by weather and climate. There are large burned surfaces in which later, smaller ones can be seen, the water's smooth surface that ripples when something is thrown in it. On my lips too, scar tissue forms on scar tissue, sections that had theoretically grown back together repeatedly tear apart again. Yet, some of the new tissue remains and becomes part of an older layer, like sediment deposits.

The fingertips of his right hand have been burned so often that his so-called fingerprints can't be taken. When he presses the pads of his fingertips on a light surface, black, imperfect circles without any relief remain. On the palms of his hands there are no lines or ridges that are, as they say, legible. They are dry lakes that undulate when moved.

His hands recount fires, the right more eloquently than the left. The scars overlay each other, merge, but unlike on fire maps, you can't isolate a period of time and block out the rest. On his hands, incidents have fused into a single surface. The oldest burns are from his childhood, his early adolescence, when fire was everywhere and open. On them are the burns from the time after, which he spent in 'backward regions', as they're called. Levels of civilization are measured by the extent to which open fires have disappeared. Fires you can't see are the ones to be afraid of, but a fire that has been intentionally lit must be watched. Like livestock, it needs to be carefully attended to so that it doesn't break free. If you fight against it, it will take its revenge. Hence the term fire fighters.

He has been an unhappy city dweller for years, without a fireplace, hearth or torch. The fresh burn blisters always on his hands are caused by hot pots and the little blue flames; the gas stove is the only fire he's allowed to have in his flat. On the inside of his right forearm, a wide plaster covers a fresh wound. He was standing in front of the range, stirring a pot on one of the back burners for a while before he noticed that the front burner under his right arm was also lit.

The community has been informed that someone has settled into the castle. No notification of lodging accommodation has been filed. If the owners can't be reached, something will have to be done. I cross the dark courtyard, a light in the workshop, like car headlights, already gone when I look over at the front gate which is closed.

At this moment, fires are being born everywhere in the world—from an ember hidden under foliage, deep in the woods, in a hollow tree trunk, a small flame from a cable behind an armoire, in the housing of a motor, in the dark. In bright midday, a sickle, stuck in a thatched roof and forgotten. A child lighting thin twigs and thicker branches with dry, slender matches. The child knows that he's only allowed to play this game in the fireplace, that outside the fireplace you don't play with fire. The adults explain the rules of handling fire, but no one says anything later about how flames can spread from the oven, out from under the cauldron. The child understands that fire is being treated unfairly and says nothing.

Before going to sleep, I open both casements of the window so that nothing will get caught in it, but when I open my eyes, a light is hovering in the courtyard. Or a reflection, like pebbles or white flowers at night. Through the bedroom, the space between the kitchen, the draught between the open door and the small window. When I stand on the doorstep and see the white phlox in the courtyard, it, too, is moving in the wind, she stands before me, faster than I can look. Our eyes at the same height, hers wide-open so that I'd fall in before I can grab onto anything. By chance, my hand is on the door, and I grab for it, pull it closed between us, slam it shut, the key is in the lock, I turn it. Inside, cloth covers the glass, thank God, visual protection, they call it. Dishevelled hair ablaze. No memory of his mother's face, who pulled him from sleep and his bed and took him away. A light figure, something white.

There are three screens in the watchman's lodge that are arranged to make the footage from all the security cameras visible at once. The screen on the right shows fire maps of the American airspace authorities, the middle screen shows European ones. The screen on the left alternately shows Australian fire maps and various smaller regional ones. The language on all maps is English, but he likes the German word 'Feuerkarte', which no one uses besides him. He begins with an overview of the earth, selects a zero cloud cover setting, without labels or borders, Blue Marble, the most appealing setting that must be used with great care. The danger lies in the loftiness. He sweeps his eyes over the beautiful wide world that is, in large stretches, covered with flames. At least that's what's suggested by the dark-red squares, which, when viewed at this scale, connect over large surfaces and cover entire regions, territories, half-continents. The youngest fires are dark-red, none more than six hours old. If you include six to twelve hours and twelve to fourteen, the colour picture becomes denser with countless light-red and orange squares. For these same time frames, Europeans use violet, pink and red symbols.

He changes the setting, bringing in cloud cover and contaminant plumes, then zooms in under the cover onto areas in which he has a particular interest and on which map markings and human traces are now indicated. The boreal forest is shown as a green band stretching from Eurasia over to North America. Most people have no idea that their lives depend on this pine forest. The fire season in the northern hemisphere peaks in July and August, but for years now has been growing longer and has left traditional patterns behind.

On the fire map, the more you zoom into the earth's surface, the more the individual squares separate and the more landscape is revealed. Green and brown shades indicate different kinds of ground cover, from pine trees to steppe. Large sections of the boreal forest are uninhabited or sparsely populated, so they are left to burn. The ground breaks away, the earth opens into trenches and craters which are not shown on the map. The forest won't grow back, this is an ancient landscape that is perishing.

With a small red arrow, he selects individual dark-red, light-red, or orange-coloured squares and data about the respective fires appears. Longitude, latitude, satellite, detection date, brightness, fire radiative power. He copies some of the place names to look for reports, which he then doesn't read. They describe the ferocity of the fires and always include pictures. But rarely do people know how to portray the fire. Most are too frightened to see. Longitude, latitude, satellite, instrument, detection date, brightness, fire radiative power. He moves from one continent to another, looking at the landscape with the colourful squares from a great distance then again as close as possible, as if he wanted to set foot on the ground. Longitude, latitude, satellite, instrument, detection date, reliability, brightness, fire radiative power.

The illusion of getting ever-closer and being able to see ever-more, and the moment always comes when, instead of revealing itself, the landscape goes blurry. Pixels in unnatural colours that just become blurry when looked at more closely. Longitude, latitude, satellite, instrument, detection date, reliability, brightness, fire radiative power, day/night. He follows the general drift from west to east, then up to the poles and back towards the equator, always ending up at the ghost lights in the Atlantic which fool the instruments. The magnetic anomaly can't be registered in the programme, they leave them to burn in the middle of the ocean. Longitude, latitude, satellite, instrument, detection date, brightness, fire radiative power, day/night, reliability.

In the watchman's lodge, the equipment hums and his breath whistles softly. He hates the inhaler the way he hates fire maps. He can look at where the fires are burning and bring adrenaline into his blood in order to breathe. Have you ever considered doing something else, the consultant asked when he saw her the last time. Something else? Professionally, she meant. Fire gives him the oxygen he needs, he feels the warmth inside. It's never too late to change something, the consultant said. His dry cough. We became pyrophytes long ago. We can't live without fire and we will perish because of it.

This morning only a thin stream came from the bathtub faucet, then nothing; same in the kitchen. I sit against the outside wall, my door wide open so the warmth and light that fill the courtyard stream in. I look away from the blackbird in the grass to the workshop wing. A man is walking heavily, carrying something in a sack towards the field, to the orchard? I want to ask, but then he has disappeared even before he reached the back gate and I look at the blooming phlox and notice in front of it, half-overgrown with grass, a round cement cover. Using all my strength, I lift it. Naturally there's a well, back then very few houses had running water. In the archway of the back gate, I find a bucket and now understand why it has a rope attached to it. The water is surprisingly clean. After washing my face and thoroughly applying tincture to my lips, I head to the store. I buy wine, raisins, bread rolls, cigarettes and several half-litre bottles of water. Our tap water's not good enough, the owner mumbles, facing the newspapers, as I load the things into my knapsack and fill a second bag. Turned off, I say. From farther back in the store I hear his wife say goodbye, and the door closes behind me.

On the bench next to me, the open jar of raisins. I've taken a handful for myself and laid a few on the inside of the lid, but still, now and again an ant tries to climb the side and get inside. In front of its burrow, the mouse gnaws on something it's holding between its front paws, a wasp lightly scrapes tiny pieces of a raisin. I lay both palms on the raw wood of the bench. Notice that the mouse is gone. The wasp too. The scraping and buzzing sounds have stopped. The time in late afternoon when the accumulated heat of the day comes in glittering armour through the shimmering above the meadow. An ant runs off over the back of my hand. I light a cigarette, the smoke doesn't rise, it floats away in the trembling air. The sirens don't break the stillness, they break away from it.

The sirens are especially beautiful at night over the city where they have room. The asphalt and paving stones cushion the sound, it bounces off the buildings' walls and up, over the roofs. The sound effortlessly plays along the edges and up to the top of the hills to the Meteorological Institute, where he hears the song. Below, they hear the noise from a hundred throats. Lots of celebrating, they call it. When it gets dark, when the sun has set for a few hours, hours that don't bring any coolness, just a slight lowering of the temperature, people pour out from indoors, songs and laughter, yells and shrieks, screams and calls echo in the streets. Since spring, campfires and grilling have been strictly forbidden everywhere within city limits and in the outskirts. The reason that fire maps don't indicate the highest danger level throughout the country is because the deepest soil layers in some areas still show some humidity. The risk of fire is also highest there—straw, fine particles, ground cover and the shrub layer can all be set alight by a spark. The pressure readings are at unprecedented levels. Everything now is in a state we never knew.

In our latitudes, the way we handle wildfires has nothing to do with inherited practices, the collective memory of household fire is as good as extinguished. People go deep into the public forest to grill their slabs of meat. They look for the most inaccessible places in the parks and when they're discovered in one spot, they move to another. Grilling becomes an act of resistance for one part of the population, the other part talks about rationality and responsibility. At night, helicopters circle over the city and he wishes he had access to their aerial views. The forbidden fires are concealed under the thickest possible foliage, the danger of crown fires is high. The bigger the fire, the more flying sparks. People don't know that the area immediately surrounding the fire must be kept clear of any flammable material and the fire should be kept low, but they bear an ancient knowledge of its destructive power, a sense of its purifying effect. Fire transforms. What is burnt can never be restored. It holds no trace of its former structure.

Almost every night people are seriously injured or killed not only by fire. The darkness is filled with the blare of sirens and flashing blue lights. The air is saturated with howling and moaning, punctuated by bursts of laughter, and the asphalt radiates the heat of the day. In the morning hours, the unconscious are found, as are the ones with their heads bashed in. Those who have lost their sight or hearing seek help from the ambulances. In the parks and public forests, firefighters extinguish the last embers. Before, people knew that urinating or spitting in fires would not go unpunished. The sun shines on black charred surfaces and scorched crowns of trees.

There is an unusually high number of fatal drownings this year. Perhaps people go into the water because they want to reach the island that is covered in flames. For the first time in its history, the vegetation on the island next to the city is burning. Only those who have no shelter are on the streets; others sit in air-conditioned buses and trams, rarely looking out the window. Restaurant patios and outdoor cafes are enclosed in glass structures that used to be called winter gardens and are now air conditioned. The closer to the river, the more neglected the city looks. There are no buildings here, just massive gates and enormous factory yards. The industrial works have long been shuttered and ships are no longer loaded here. Some streets are still paved with old stones. A bed of withered shrubs. He stands next to it, looking at the flat, elongated island in the middle of the wide river. The flames are barely visible with the sun high in the sky, the air over the island seems liquid, the light-grey smoke indicates a ground fire. A footbridge to the island spans the water, the air grows denser with every step. He doesn't reach into his pocket for his inhaler, he wants to reach the fire and can't believe it's possible until, having climbed up to the bridge, he finds a safety gate. Danger warning and threat of punishment. He leans both arms on the railing and breathes the smoke-filled air in and out. Before him, below him, the island.

The fire is slow, deliberate, as if it knew that it only has a limited area at its disposal but also that no one would disturb it. It's there for its own sake and for him on the footbridge. It won't be put out, the responders are needed elsewhere. The access points have been closed, the fire has been left to burn out on its own. It's unlikely to spread, the sparks and burning twigs carried on the light wind burn out in mid-air or sink down and are extinguished in the water. He stretches one arm out, then the other, palms facing down, as if to warm them. The island started burning at both ends at once, arson is the presumed cause. Under the prevailing conditions, however, an unfortunate coincidence must also be taken into consideration. Fire and backfire extinguish each other, but still, no matter where they meet, anything on the island that can burn will burn. The fires advance towards each other without haste. The pedestrian and bicycle paths form a network of fire lanes but the fire itself creates the gusts that carry it over the asphalt.

There are large fields that are regularly mowed or grazed, and the fire takes hold of one stalk after another until the entire field is a silent, smouldering fire. The shrubs and low trees on the island's elevated ridge are thickly clustered, they're most exposed to the wind. Hardest to set alight are the poplars and willows on the water's edge. Once in a while, a spark manages to light a crown on fire, making the tree burn like a torch. On the fenced-in area where sheep grazed most recently, there's no fuel left, just dusty ground, sparse yellowed tufts of grass, which is why the animals were removed from the island before the fire started. The beavers had abandoned their lodges even before the fire alert and swam across the river. The cherry-tree grove in the centre of the island is untouched.

He realizes that he can't hear the fire any longer. The roar of the multilane expressway on the other side of the river drowns out even the sound of his airways. But he can feel the constriction in his throat and ribcage, the rattle and hum in his bronchial tubes and he reaches for his inhaler. Not yet. One hand in his pocket, the other on the railing, step by step, two streets farther on, he slips into the shade of a courtyard entrance. He shivers, doubles up, his entire musculature cramps, even his throat, chest and stomach, down to his lumbar. He lifts the inhaler to his lips, draws on it once, breathes in as deeply as he can, not a second time. He waits, leaning against the wall, his arms wrapped around his torso. The subway, a bus or taxi are out of the question—cold air is the worst stimulus. He walks for an hour and rests in the shade of a playground's wooden tower. He lifts the inhaler to his lips, one puff, inhales, waits. He walks another hour and rests again in an entryway, then finally reaches his flat. Stretched out on the couch, head and neck supported, leaving his respiratory muscles as unconstrained as possible. No pills today. That night he sleeps deeply and soundly, as they say, for eight hours. Almost like surviving twice.

I didn't get a wink of sleep, held onto something from the moment I got up, the bed frame, the marble top of the dresser, the cloth on the floor. I wash with the water I collected from the well yesterday. I walk through the kitchen, my hand on the sideboard, on the stove. I make coffee with water from the bottle. Earlier they drank the well water. Now I sit in the courtyard, on the chair near the front door, my back firmly against the wall.

Every morning, I step outside and every morning it's bright, even when the sun is still low, even when it hasn't risen yet. As soon as night starts to give way, it's bright, dry and windless. The catastrophes aren't the howling winds and thundering storms, the end is dead calm. No converging or changes in air masses, everything stalled. The dish cloth on the chair back is just as I hung it yesterday, the dried flower petals on the crown of the wall haven't blown away, nor have the seeds and capsules on the plants. I crave a wind that would lift my hair and refresh my cheeks, make them red and warm without sweat. I want to shrug my shoulders against the cold and rub my frigid hands together.

If war were to break out in this season, target practice would be enough to start a major fire and Europe would go up in flames. As if of a piece, as they say. You need fire to cast, he says. The wildfires will spread faster than talk of war. No matter exactly when it starts, it will last until the next fire season and beyond. I'm sitting on the bench by the back gate, in the midday sun, which should be avoided, which makes you sleepy, which reflects and blurs the atmospheric layers and closes distance. The birches play a dizzying game, create a breeze in their foliage even when there's no wind, so that their leaves dazzle and flash.

I go to the window and am holding the handle when a gust of wind snatches it and pushes it into the room, blowing full in my face, which I raise abruptly. Sweat drips down the groove under my nose and into the wounds on my lips. It burns. I stand up so I can apply the tincture and then go across the fields and into the woods. In southern France, a vast area, a military compound, has been burning for three days. Firefighting operations are difficult because of the ammunition depot. The officer responsible for the target practice is brought before a military court. In earlier times, the law in many places condemned arsonists and fire looters to burn at the stake. They were burned, of course, what else?

He likes to contemplate the burning in his intestines. He pictures a pure fire. No flame, but a colourless glow that spreads in all directions as warmth does. The fire expands slowly, very slowly, it consumes him from inside until nothing is left. An incineration without residue. No soot particles glowing orange–yellow, no harmful emissions, no little pile of ashes. All his life energy in the form of warmth and light offered to the air. The mountain has dissolved into air.

On the edge of the forest, I look around before I plunge in. First a short, slow run, testing my muscles and tendons, then faster. The soles of my feet feel the ground, leaves, branches, vines, needles, soft earth, the degree of give. One ankle adapts, under no circumstances can it sprain, my other foot needs to be there already, to compensate. I stop, listen, go on at the right moment, not knowing what my body is doing, surrendering myself. Up a slope, the last step a leap onto an unknown top and beyond, then I stand still, trembling from the effort. I search for a view, examine the landscape, ditches, forest aisles, the spots where they might be crossed, roads to avoid. Bare cliffs, inaccessible escarpments, every pond, pool, stream, there's not much water. It's especially important to keep track of cardinal directions and wind conditions.

A wooden hut on stilts at the highest point of the landscape. The vast expanses of forests are gone now, as is the profession of fire watcher. The last lookout in the celebrated national park was a writer who described the fires but didn't alert anyone. He was let go. In this country, sensors have been mounted on old fire watchtowers and mobile phone masts. One sensor covers more than a hundred thousand hectares, reports the smallest irregularities, smoke or dust. Somewhere, someone sits and monitors the images.

In the Meteorological Institute, in the middle of the night, he leaves the watchman's lodge, climbs the broad staircase in the main building, three storeys, the halls to the offices lit with emergency lighting, no one else is in the building. A low steel door and behind it a narrow circular staircase, high steps, a tower from the century before last, he steps out onto the roof. At the top of four steps, a thin ladder to the highest point, the walled platform with the measuring instruments. The river is not in the range of vision; it runs through the plain on the other side of the hill. In the morning, he'll finish his shift, cross the hill crest, and descend to the city. Since the island started burning, he only looks at the fire maps when he can't be on the footbridge. On the maps, he avoids looking at the island fire.

No one understands how the fire can possibly still be burning there. The estimates were that the fire would have consumed all the dried vegetation within a few days and fresh grass would grow from the ash-fertilized ground. Instead, the area has continued burning for an inexplicably long time, destroying ever-deeper layers of the soil. The smoke hangs over the city and blends with the reddish yellow dust. There was an unexpected outbreak in the Sahara. There's a grating in his lungs, the inhaler is no help for that.

The deer come when the light dims, when the sun has set, and you could believe that the sky is overcast. Electric light does not dispel the darkness from the houses and you can see how light it still is when you're outside. The deer approach from the forest edge and the fields. They enter the gardens where there's no fence or there's a hole in the fence, a way through. As long as they don't move, they're invisible. I, too, have stopped moving. A deer looks at me from the circular rose bed in a driveway. When I move again, it lowers its head and continues grazing.

I walk steadily, the path descends between two hillsides, rises again, it's no longer far to the castle. A blast and then another. On the slope to my right a movement, grey or light-brown on an ochre background, rapid, like a glide, diagonally across the field, into the hollow, where our paths cross. I pick up my pace to the point of intersection. The bleating of sheep and human cries, a man's voice and a woman's down there! A blast and then another. I hurry up the opposite slope, continuing the line across the field, away from the voices, towards the forest.

The ploughed earth gets heavier with each step, running on all fours, shoulder blades rising and falling with each step. Howls behind me, I have to throw off the pelt I'm wearing. I tug at the sheet I've thrown over myself, lie on my stomach, breathing heavily. My hands tremble as I cling to the metal bars above my head.

On the phone my sister tells me that her child has recovered from the respiratory illness and is starting to talk. Soon her child will be able to say more than I can. My sister laughs. How's your wound? I look out over the field and make my affirming sound. In late afternoon, it's often the light that brings back memories. Through the window I saw something fall from the sky and drop on the ground not far from the tree. It was black, about the size of a crow. I went out, in front of the house he suddenly appeared next to me. The creature was gone, but near the tree we found a trap. We pushed a stick between the open serrated jaws. It's the same light, but the animal was on the other side, the side near the street where there's no tall tree. My sister asks if I'm coming back anytime.

There are at least four hearths in the castle. A fireplace in the room between the kitchen and the bedrooms, the old stove which is as clean as the fireplace—dusty, but free of soot or ash—and there's the oven that I saw through the window in the workshop building, as well the oven with the cauldron in the orchard. This morning the electric range and the lamps stopped working and the radiator won't turn on either. In the shop, I put several bottles of water, candles, lighters, matches and a gas canister in a shopping basket. At the counter, I order three rolls. The owner's wife holds the small paper bag with the rolls over the counter but doesn't hand it to me. What've you got there? she asks softly and hurriedly. From the register in the front of the store come the loud voices of a customer who is hard of hearing and the owner. His wife looks at my lips and returns my look. A wound, I say. But for a long time now, she says. It's not healing. She hands me the rolls. I pay her husband at the register. He says nothing and the customer looks on in silence.

Watch out, they'll run you out of town as a witch. I'm now in the region with the highest danger level in the country. We don't have 'extreme' here, just 'elevated'. The warning system has still not been adapted to the changed circumstances. The reason is that more data is needed. The supervisor hasn't come to the watchman's lodge in a long time. He's urgently looking for specialists in forest fire algorithms.

Tonight, the draught in my bedroom is stronger than usual. I look at the door that leads I don't know where, but it's still closed. I get up, walk through the passage with the fireplace, across the kitchen and the courtyard, the draught accompanying me. When I slow my steps, it retreats, when I stop, it's gone. I walk with calm steps so that even when it's faint, I can feel the draught on my left side. Out the back gate and into the field. The hill ridge behind which the glowing red sun sank a few hours ago. Now the flames are closer, halfway here. I know the horizon depends on my perspective and that distances are most deceptive in the dark.

It's made up of several small fires, I hear the crackling, the whistling of the gases from the wood, the flames singing. At any moment, these fires could joint into a front and start to advance. A wind could rise, it was a draught that brought me outside. There are unsettled spots in the fire, a single tall flame that detaches itself and moves off, hovers, an invisible body carries it over the field towards me. I'm immobilized and the flame suddenly racing. Just when it is about to cross the ditch, I catch sight of a pair of glowing eyes, then they're gone, as if swallowed up by the night. The fires on the field burn sedately and reddish yellow. The smoke isn't visible in the darkness. I wait for the figure to reappear.

The fire maps indicate measurements that will be spread hundreds and thousands of kilometres by sensors, antennae and cables. He has studied the numbers, he knows the critical levels, he knows to combine the meteorological data on temperature, wind, precipitation and relative humidity with the pertinent data on land cover and the fuel moisture codes of the litter and other fine fuels as well as for upper and deeper organic materials in order to calculate the aggregate fire danger. But when he sits motionless before the screens, without clicking on the boxes with data, letting his gaze rest on the alienated landscape, it sometimes pulls him to a certain place where there is nothing to see, where there's possibly not even cause to find an elevated risk, from which he can't tear himself away. A bodily disquiet. A feeling. He keeps an eye on the spot, often for days at a time, until at some point a red square appears. He has never told anyone about this.

Before closing the jar, I scatter a handful of raisins in front of the mouse's hole. Since I arrived, the mouse could have raised one generations of offspring and borne a second. Dusk has fallen when I make my way through the front gate. The municipality is celebrating the end of summer, and I've cleaned myself up. I've put on a pair of dark trousers and a matching shirt and noticed that all my clothes have tiny holes and uneven edges, not from fire, but gnawed away by the mice I sometimes hear scurrying and rustling in the bedroom. I've applied the tincture generously on my upper and lower lips, inside and out. Several villages are part of the municipality, the celebration is being held at some distance from the castle, behind the old firehouse that now stands empty because the fire departments were merged several years ago. The volunteers come from all villages, the control centre is in the largest one, some distance from here.

I approach in a large arc, taking the field path up to the forest edge, which I follow towards the fairground. I look at it from above. There are cars parked everywhere, one field on the other side of the road serves as a parking area, the sound system reverberates through the surroundings. The fairground consists of booths, a wooden grandstand and many beer benches. Behind it, on the field next to the hillside, near the forest edge, they've built the bonfire. The firemen started it two weeks ago, skilfully building a pile several metres high; it would have made for a beautiful fire. Up until the last minute, people had hoped it would rain before the festival, this morning they surrounded it with red-white-red barrier tape. The traditional fire had to be cancelled due to the high fire hazard.

From the forest edge I see the bonfire pile looming darkly, the illuminated fairground behind it. There's dancing, the sound and stamping waft up to me. They stopped burning straw figures years ago and no one remembers the custom in which young people jumped over the fire after it had burned down. The last ones who still knew that being untouched by fire signified infertility died a long time ago.

Two people are sitting against the back wall of a booth and drinking out of half-litre mugs with a view of the bonfire and the hill behind it. In the darkness, the faint glow of a cigarette. The castle burned once before. Even if the insurance paid, something there isn't right. No water and no electricity. There must be several of them there, a nest of them, at night you can hear voices. They should get rid of it, tear it down, build something new.

Maps drawn by North Americans also show gas flares used in oil extraction, coal mining or in chemical processing. In the eastern part of this country, there are light-red and yellow squares, the refinery is less than one hundred kilometres from here. Protective suits, hoses, tanker trucks: a lot of combustion is needed for firefighting. Most of the vegetation fires are started or caused by humans, the presence of human infrastructure is often the decisive factor for fire hazard. European maps only show vegetation fires. On their maps the land is immersed in deep darkness. The two people have disappeared from the back wall of the booth. Fire regimes have only applied in times of peace, that is, as long as individual communities have held together.

A figure steps out of the illuminated sphere of the fairground and walks towards the bonfire to the adjacent cornfield, and squats down. Farther up, another figure now nears the one who is squatting and looking down at the festival grounds; the squatter hears steps approaching and bolts up, trying to pull up their trousers, breaks into a run. The other figure catches up and both fall to the ground in one dark mass.

There is someone standing next to the bonfire, lighting a cigarette. The booths and the wooden grandstand are abandoned in the darkness, a light wind moves the crop on the fields and makes the flames flicker slightly. Because the bonfire was cancelled, no preparations had been made—the surrounding area was not watered nor cleared of any fire loading. The sparks fall on fertile ground. Fleet-footed, the fire runs across the stubble field, down to the fairground and up the hill towards the forest edge.

I descend the hill on the darkened field path and into the village. I step onto the brightly lit street, dazzled, suddenly on hard surface. My legs give way and I fall. I prop myself up. Spit. People outside their front doors, in their front gardens, they're no longer looking at the glow of the fire on the horizon. I crouch in the middle of the street and spit, not just blood. Stand up, spit again, there are small bits in my mouth. No one comes near me. I walk away. I leave.

In the castle, I wash my newly split lips with water from the well, then with bottled water. I disinfect them with fruit brandy and hold cloth to the wound. When the bleeding slows, I see in the hand mirror that the stitches have come loose. There's no surgical thread in either my upper or lower lip. Burning, reddened eyes, blackened face, an open mouth smiles at me.

The crackling and rustling are transmitted directly to the skin. A chimney fire or campfire can't even come close to sounding like a wildfire. It breathes as it consumes the wood, one piece after another, it makes you hungry, makes you want to eat, to devour. Sometimes English words are the most suited to fire. Canopy means baldachin, firmament, leaf canopy and forest cover. Kneeling in front of the stove, he takes a deep breath to blow on the embers. From his ribcage comes less of a rattle than a cooing, the flames leap up and begin humming. From a medical point of view, he should avoid any contact with fire. I watch as he draws breath and gives it to the fire. The fire makes a high whistling sound and from deep in his throat comes a soft, melodic, twittering from his lower respiratory tract, a polyphonic singing. I sit on the kitchen bench with one leg pulled up. He stands, leaning against the stove. Don't, I say, when he moves to support himself with his palms behind him and he crosses his arms in front of this chest.

In the middle of the night, it's quiet all around. We've eaten, consumed piece by piece, then waited for the fire to die down, until the embers have gone out as well. In former times, fire was covered at night, put to bed. The day began with waking it, rekindling the embers in the ashes, between pieces of coal. We still have lighters and matches left. We'll rub sticks between our hands, we'll lay paper under glass in the sun, we'll try everything to create sparks, to warm and feed ourselves and keep away wild animals. He uncrosses his arms. Comes up to me and lays his warm hand on my bare knee. We can stay here for a while, not for long. The bird in his chest sometimes perches higher up and sometimes on the ground below, like now, close to my mouth.